JACKO MORAN
sniper

JACKO MORAN
sniper

Ken Catran

Lothian
BOOKS

Thomas C. Lothian Pty Ltd
132 Albert Road, South Melbourne, Victoria 3205
www.lothian.com.au

National Library of Australia
Cataloguing-in-Publication data:

Catran, Ken.
Jacko Moran : sniper.

For young adults.
ISBN 0 7344 0551 0.

I. Title.

NZ823.2

Cover and text illustrations by Declan Lee
Cover design by Ranya Langenfelds
Text design by Paulene Meyer
Printed in Australia by Griffin Press

To the memory of Siegfried Sassoon whose poems brought alive the horror of war.

My thanks to the Waiouru Army Museum and to the Frank Sargeson, Buddle Findlay Trust for their assistance in the development of this novel.

Flanders poppies

New Zealand, 1940

I'M NOT IN the hospital. I'm back in the war.

The mists clear. Smoke from the shells, it's white, maybe phosphorus, so be careful. And through it come the Germans, on the attack again. Good soldiers, maybe more of those new divisions from the Eastern Front. We are firing, they fall but keep coming.

One man, the metal tank on his back, long hose-pipe in his hands. Flammenwerfer! *I spit the mud from my lips, sight the Mannlicher, the rifle-butt cold against my sweating cheek. Narrow my eyes to the stinging smoke, squeeze the trigger, work the bolt and fire again.*

The captain yelling, ignore him, fire a third time. Yes! The flamethrower man spins around, explodes in greedy orange flames. German soldier, killed by a German bullet from my German rifle. Crazy bloody war! Dead, quickly and horribly, but there are many horrible ways to die in the trenches. Captain Couch is yelling again. This time I let myself listen.

'Moran! Gas!'

Gas! Jerk the container around, my movement limited because the German snipers have me targeted. The yellow clouds forming, the greasy sweetish taste on my

7

lips, harshly tickling into my throat. I have to breathe in, feel it go to my lungs, slap the gas-mask on, hope I have not breathed too much.

Picking up my rifle again, peering through the large Perspex eyeholes, misting already. Western Front. My old man cracked on what a street-fighter he was, wouldn't have lasted five minutes here.

Are you listening to this, Dad?

'I'm listening.'

And I'm not in that stinking muddy shell-hole any more, choking on gas fumes. I'm in the cold hospital night, disinfectant; the neat white sheets up to my chin and my lungs on fire because I've been coughing.

Dad is at the end of the bed and moves forward, dragging one leg. Sure, a packing case fell on his foot, but he limps for the free drinks.

'You're dying, son.'

'You died twenty-odd years ago.'

He's as I remember him. Tall, pot-bellied, greasy long hair and always that nasty set to his lips. I-give-a-rats-arse-for-nobody. He never did for his wife or kids. I don't want him here, so blink my eyes open and he's gone.

Quick footsteps now, belonging to Nurse Tanner. Face like a camel, righteous grey eyes and set mouth; but she's cared for me more than most others did. Except Jessica … and Betty. Eileen!

'Try not to cough too hard, Mr Moran, it only makes things worse. Would you like some water?'

'Thanks.'

I don't really want any. But I do want her touch, to believe someone cares. She raises my head, I sip the water. It can't put out the fire in my lungs.

'Try and sleep, Mr Moran.'

She's ice cool, there's no warmth in her words. She walks back to her desk at the end of the ward and I count her footsteps. Seventeen. I was that age when I joined up.

My name is Robert Moran, my mates called me 'Jacko.' I am forty-three years old and dying. The doc says weak lungs and pneumonia; really, the mustard gas they never gave me a pension for.

I was one of those 'boy soldiers' of the Great War, although now they are calling it 'World War One'; served at Gallipoli and on the Western Front. Four years of unending nightmare but, looking back now, the only years I really lived. All the mates who called me 'Jacko' are dead now, ghosts. Brasso, Duncan, Harry, even old Hooter. Frog and Pig, best double act ever on a Vickers gun.

Good officers, like Rowlands and Couch. Bad ones like Creel — and he's no ghost, sod him. But he remembers me every time he sits down, ha ha.

A voice comes from nowhere. 'Look at you, Jacko, idle bugger. Fancy a quick game?'

'With you? Still know the back of a deck of cards better than the front?'

Brasso grins. That sleeveless leather jacket of his undone, muddy from head to foot, helmet cocked back.

'You can't dodge this one, Jacko. Old Man Death's a better sniper than you.'

'Sod off, you bloody card-sharp.'

Then I cough again, the mists close like gunsmoke, I see Duncan. He smiles at me, no hard feelings, Sorry mate, talk to you later. Dead, like all my mates, buried if we found the bodies —

'Jacko?'

For a moment I don't want to see her. Then turn my head a little and see that grey uniform skirt of hers. She smiles, cigarette in the corner of her mouth; her eye puckers at the smoke.

'Hello, Jessica.'

A bloody good nurse. Harry's girl, but a Turk sniper got him at Gallipoli. Dark-haired, good-looking and tough; to nurse as long as she did, you have to be. Her voice is gentle.

'You know you are dying, Jacko.'

'I should have died then, eh, in Flanders?' I choke back another cough in case it brings Nurse Tanner. 'While I was still a cow-cakes sergeant.'

Her touch puts out that sandpaper fire in my lungs. Her eyes are cool too, and full of caring. That smile of hers.

'Where the hell are we, Jacko?'

Jessica, I'm in Wellington hospital, but I know what you mean. It's just over twenty years on and we're fighting like hell to stop the Huns — again. Twenty-odd years after the war to end all wars, Hitler's planes are bombing London *and his troops are all over Europe. Like the Somme, Ypres and Passchendaele never happened.*

But they did happen. So did the end of the war and the impossible trick of turning soldiers into civilians. And the Great Depression also happened. Then this hospital happened and Jessica Collingwood, who died of influenza in 1918, is beside me. At least the pain is gone.

'You've got a few hours, Jacko. No more pain.'

'What am I supposed to do with a few hours?'

It's funny talking like this. Words on closed lips, people who are real when I shut my eyes. Jessica here, like a dream before you wake up. Her firm hand on mine.

'Think about your life, Jacko. I did. The sum total, you know?'

Sum total? I open my eyes again — or do I close them? — and she is there, her smile a little sad now. She will stay. Maybe Eileen would have but I cannot call to her. Or Betty Donaghy, because the living won't come.

Jessica's speaking again. 'I'm sorry about you and Betty.'

The sum total of my life was four years in Gallipoli and Flanders. Years of stinking horror and tension, kill or be killed in the corpse-ridden, cratered, black jungle of no-man's land at night. They should have been the worst years of my life. And they were.

They were the only years I really lived.

Flanders, 1916

Mademoiselle from Armentières, parlez-vous...

—soldiers' song

I SHOULD START in England. The big training camp at Shoreditch where we got the works, rifle-drill, square-bashing. Lots of new guys in our battalion who'd never seen a shot fired in anger. I met Eileen there — *think about her later!*

Then getting crammed on some British steamer and shipped across to France. I remember the sharp, salt smell, the fog and those bloody foghorns —

'Cripes, they make a noise,' says Brasso beside me. 'Think the Hun submarines will hear?'

'They'll still have to bloody find us.'

The fog is so thick, I can scarcely see Brasso. He must have won his poker game to be up on deck. It's better than the close sweaty below-decks and over-worked toilets. The foghorn blares again. On my other side a man elbows to the rail, the black cat badge of the Cumberland Borderers on his greatcoat.

'Can't even smoke,' he says, pronouncing it 'smeke'. 'As if Hoons (Huns) could see in this pea-soup.'

The deck is crowded with soldiers, huddled in their greatcoats, speaking in low mutters. Not thinking about submarines but about where they are going.

'Mook, lice, rats and Hoons, here ah coom,' growls the Black Cat man. 'Second time. First time was mah worse when bloody soobmarine got them Navy ships.'

He tells us, though we don't want to listen. It seems this Hun submarine torpedoed a Navy cruiser.

So another Navy cruiser arrives and stops to take on survivors. So the Hun submarine slaps a torpedo in her ribs. So yet another Navy cruiser steams up and stops — yes, and she cops one too. They all sink.

'Bloody stupid Navy,' he mutters. 'Had to learn the hard way.'

Brasso brings out a little silver flask — poker winnings — and we take a swallow each. The Black Cat soldier belches with satisfaction.

'So have the generals learned to fight this war?' asks Brasso.

The soldier takes a fag-end from behind his ear. Remembers the no-smoking rule and pitches it over-side. He grins at us, without humour.

'Them boogers? Aye, when pigs shyte diamonds.'

The foghorns sound again.

Tippety-tap tap tap, tippety-tap-tap-tap.

And our boots clop-clopping on the *pavé*, to the beat of the drum. *Pavé*, French name for road, good roads too, stood up well to the German shellfire. And the songs we sang until the dust caked in our throats. 'Tipperary' and 'Siegfried Line', with some rude add-ons.

Dust swirling, little red flowers by the roadside; an old farmer dressed in black, leaning on his stick and watching us. Mainly women working on the farms, too busy to bother. They'd seen too many soldiers pass. Some of the young ones give us a look and get one back.

Eighty pounds on our backs and the straps rubbing our shoulders raw. Hot as hell in the heavy khaki uniforms. The leather straps of our rifles squeaking. Sweat is streaming down our faces and the canteens are dry. *Estaminet* is the second French word we learn. *Vin* is the first. Our tongues are hanging out for the nearest *estaminet* to buy some *vin*.

'Keep your section closed, corporal!' shouts our new sergeant, a red-faced tub called McKinnon. We picked him up when the battalion re-formed in Egypt after Gallipoli. I was acting-sergeant but never saw eye to eye with Captain Creel, so that was that.

'Pig!' I shouted. 'Stop gawping at them kids!'

'Pig', otherwise Private Frank Hogge, has tossed some chocolate to some kids. They jabber back at him, laughing. He's roasted with sunburn, cheeks pitted with acne, and tufty brown hair under his helmet.

'Them kids speak French well, don't they, corp?'

'Well, they're bloody French, of course they do,' says Newton, another new boy.

Pig nods. 'That's what I mean, like it's natural with them.'

Newton just sighs and keeps plodding. It's too hot to argue. And Pig thinks everyone in France speaks English and has to learn French. Mind you, he's straight off the farm and the sheep have more brains.

A lot of new boys in our platoon. Appleyard, Connor, Bright, Bingham — a clown. Only Duncan and Brasso left of the old platoon at Gallipoli, and that's because they were wounded and shipped back to Egypt.

'We can cut the dust tonight, corp,' says Brasso with a wink.

'Brasso' because he has the sheer brass nerve to get away with anything — including some wine at the last village, and the officers saw nothing.

'Fall out!' comes the shout. 'Ten minutes!'

Brasso mops his forehead with a blue polka-dot handkerchief. 'At least we're in a civilised country,' he says. 'Not like that soddin' graveyard.'

He means Gallipoli and Anzac Cove. Maybe, but some civilised Huns are waiting at the end of this march to give us an uncivilised reception. And right then, like I'd wished it, we hear something.

There's a nice little breeze, cool on our hot faces. It changes and now comes a low distant mutter; sort of faint grumble like an empty stomach wanting food. I know that noise, it makes me tingle.

Guns.

'Like old times,' says Duncan, puffing on his cigarette. Fair-haired and skinny, good hand with a bayonet. Used to be a butcher.

Yes, old times. The front line, still a fair march away but waiting for us. And then we'll be right back in the war.

'Sounds like the war's still there,' says Rowlands.

Our company lieutenant, green as a cabbage, but all right. He makes a few jokes, plainly thinks that's what an officer should do. Save your breath, mate, I think, long way to go yet and no jokes at the end.

Creel comes trotting up, face pinker than usual in the heat. I say 'trotting' because he's got a horse from somewhere. Captain Rupert Creel is never one to rough it. He even came over on a better ship, not the old rust-bucket they crammed us into.

A glance at me as he dismounts. Creel often glances at me and I know why. At Gallipoli, we lost Harry Wainwright, a good mate, when Creel ordered a patrol that should never have taken place. He's gutless, too, and I told the yellow maggot what I thought of him. He was a useless bloody lieutenant then. He's a useless bloody captain now.

That glance got me reduced back to corporal and every dirty job he could land on me. Clever with it, and not too obvious, because we do have better officers (thank God) and senior to him.

'We'll bivouac at the next village, lieutenant,' he says to Rowlands, slapping his breeches with his riding crop. 'Then an easy step to the front.' He's pitching his voice higher for us to hear. 'Looking forward to coming to grips with the Hun, eh?'

You won't be, I think. Creel found lots of reasons to be out of the front line at Gallipoli; it'll be no different here. Everything comes second to saving his stinking yellow hide. I don't hear Rowlands' reply.

The bivouac is good news. We're all bloody tired.

TINNED STEW, tea, and army biscuit for dinner that night. We're billeted around the back of a farm and the French owner eyes us like we're after his pig. His wife has rounded up the hens and geese and locked them in the house. Smart move, but Brasso had already scored one. We trade a few francs for some of their long loaves and get down to cooking it.

The grumble of guns is closer.

Where I came from, we never ate geese. Duncan's a good cook but it's a greasy meat. Our last quiet meal for some time. Eighteen in our platoon and the goose doesn't go far, nor does the bottle of wine, and we take turns.

I kick Brasso's foot and we wander off quietly around the barn. Out comes the second bottle and we take turns.

'How's your shoulder?'

'Hurting like hell, corp. Light duties only?'

'Get stuffed.'

Brasso stopped a Mauser bullet early at Gallipoli, otherwise he might not be here to steal wine. Took his bullet in the shoulder but they patched him up in Alexandria. He's a card-sharp, a street-boy like me and the best thief in the battalion. Big nose, black hair clipped short, always looks a bit cross-eyed, and crafty as hell.

Duncan joins us. Trust him to suss the other bottle. He got a gut-wound and they are the worst. Good soldier still, but I keep an eye on him. I think that Turk bullet bust something else too. I hope I'm wrong.

We can see distant lights where the grumbling is, flares or shell-bursts. A flight of planes goes droning overhead.

'How the hell do they find their way at night?' says Duncan, squinting upward.

'Who cares?' grunts Brasso. 'Go on, you muckers, bomb the hell out of Fritz and save us a job.'

Sergeant McKinnon comes up and we just have time to hide the bottle. 'Moran, you're on first sentry-go,' he snaps. Of course I am, with Creel pulling the strings. 'Move it.'

So I get my rifle and take up my position. I never really wanted stripes, but damned if I'll let Creel find an excuse to take them off me.

I think. The wine leaves a sharp, sour taste on my lips. Eight thousand of us killed or wounded at Gallipoli for sweet bloody nothing. We're fighting Huns now, along with half a million others, and Gallipoli was just a sideshow. Eight thousand casualties in a single hour sometimes, and Flanders will be like nothing else. Trench warfare at its worst, the old lags tell us.

We'll see. I'm a sniper, so designated. I used to stalk in no-man's land and trade bullets with the Turk snipers. They were good so I had to be better. At least it got me out of trench duties and I liked it. I was in control.

There's a burst of laughter from the lighted farmhouse. The officers are making a night of it. Major Fields is good, thinks I'm an insolent bugger. Well, I am, but I know how to fight and kill. Wish my bloody dad could see me now.

And I like the army. It's a damn sight better than shovelling coal at the railyards, boots out at the toes, and drunk Dad grabbing my pay whenever he could; two sisters, our mum dead from some coughing sickness.

So I've got something better now. And the Huns will have to be bloody good, because Jacko Turk was the best. And I was 'Jacko-Hunter', because I was better than them. That's how I got my nickname. So I ground my rifle and listen to the distant guns. I can almost smell gunsmoke.

Tomorrow.

Join the army! I can remember how the old bugger laughed.

Lee Enfield and Mauser rifles

'YOU WANT to enlist, son? Do your bit for King and Country? What in blazes has King and Country ever done for you?'

'I just want to join the bloody army, Dad.'

'Oh, I don't know about that, son, don't know about that at all. You're under-age — got to be eighteen, don't you?'

'I can pass for eighteen easy. And I don't give a muckers what you think.'

'You're under-age son, it's not right. I'm your dad and I have my say.'

'When did you ever give a tinker's cuss about me?'

'Always a first time, son. What sort of earner is it?'

'Dunno, maybe two bob a day.'

'Cripes — that all! Here, you've got some set aside from the railyards, eh?'

'So?'

'So I hope you're leaving some for your old man.'

'Booze money?'

'A couple of quid sounds fair. Then I forget I'm your dad.'

'You forgot that years ago.'

'Two quid or you don't join.'

'Here. I hope it chokes you.'

'Ha ha! The army must be bloody hard up. You silly bugger, you'll get your mucking head shot off.'

Kitchener poster

PING! A TINY bit of shrapnel on my head, the shell must have exploded some distance away because it just bounces off. Ping! Another.

Not exactly on my head, on my helmet. No helmets at Gallipoli, the generals thought they were unsoldierly. We'd collapse our caps by taking out the wire reinforcing, making them less of a target.

Now — after enough head wounds — they've decided we can have them. Bowl-shaped with a flat brim, no cover for the face, but better than nothing.

We are close to the front line. An artillery duel is on at the moment, our eighteen-pounders against their 77mms. The bigger 5.9s haven't joined in so maybe it's nothing special. Maybe they know we are replacing the Poms and have laid on a welcome. Nice of them.

Anyway the air is full of noise and thunder and bits of iron from shrapnel exploding overhead, with yellow clouds wreathing around and the bitter, familiar smell of cordite. I sniff it almost with welcome, like the cooking fires of home. Maybe this is home for me. We tramp on, heads down and shoulders hunched, like when the rain sleets in your face.

It has been raining and the trenches are slippery with mud. The sun's behind overcast clouds today. Now we are passing through the second line and into the communication saps. 'Capillaries leading to the main arteries,' jokes Rowlands, ducks as a shell screams overhead. Arteries carry blood and trenches spill it, nice joke, Mr Rowlands.

Front line mate, nothing to laugh at there!

Near the front line now. The trenches are deep, well-cut and zig-zag. Lined with sandbags, the odd body-part sticking out where bodies were buried with them. Gallipoli trenches used to be squishy underfoot for the same reason. Always a hand or two sticking out; the routine is to pause and shake it.

'Gidday mate, how are you?'

Brasso next, never mind the hand is swollen, black and flabby. 'Hope you were a staff officer,' he says politely.

Some scared grins from the new boys. Pig makes to take the hand and thinks twice. If he lasts a week, he'll be ignoring worse than that.

Now the trench stink hits me, familiar as gun-smoke. That smell of mud and filth and bodies; too many bodies, all rotting. No-man's land is a cemetery of the unburied dead.

A shell bursts right overhead, fragments slash into a sandbag beside me. Creel is shouting orders, his voice gabbles high; busy working on his excuse to go to the rear, I'll bet. Late afternoon and a flare goes up from the Hun lines, red as blood. The shellfire seems heavier.

'Looks like they're pleased to see us,' shouts Rowlands. His face pale, a hand on his helmet like keeping his hat on in a storm. He's showing guts, we like that. Creel is keeping well to the shelter of the trench.

Now British troops are lined up, looking the way we will in a few days' time. Plastered with muck from head to toe, uniforms in tatters; good soldiers though, equipment and rifle clean. The duckboards squelch underfoot, the shells scream overhead. Wide white grins on their mud-masked faces.

'Left the kettle on for you, Fernleaf.'

'Give Fritz hot pepper, only way to teach him.'

'Careful of the rats, big as horses, they are.'

'Good luck, boys, God save you.'

This last from a white-whiskered army padre, clasping his Bible. Newton crosses himself and gets a glower; the padre's a Protestant. Another soldier ahead at an angle, shouting something we *all* listen to.

''Ware fixed rifle, 'ware, lads, duck damned low.'

Fixed rifle, a point in the trench that the Huns have sighted. Bingham the clown sticks his helmet over it, torn from his hand a moment later; drilled with a large puckered hole. He ducks lower than us all, straightens to find my fist in his face.

'That's coming out of your pay, smart-arse.'

No more grins and jokes as he picks up his helmet. The others follow, ducking very low indeed. Creel looks very pasty, takes a gulp from his flask before heading for a dugout. Rowlands looks after him, he's getting Creel's measure now. We go on to our sector.

A platoon-sized length of trench. Bombproof dugouts set into the sandbagged walls, firing points for two light machine-guns and one heavy. McKinnon lets me place the men, me on the heavy Vickers with Brasso as loader. It's nearly dark, the shellfire is dying away. A last one bursts and Newton yells as shrapnel slices through his arm. Our first casualty.

I stick a field-dressing on, it'll be painful but will only keep him out of the front line a couple of weeks. He's green enough to whisper, 'Bad luck, eh?' He'll soon get over that.

We are near a mortar section and that *is* bad news. Hun artillery always target mortars and may overshoot. The dugouts are good though, roofed with corrugated-iron and sandbags, the trench dug to below head level, with a firing step running along. It's dark now and the sentries are posted.

Pig and Duncan. I'm watching Duncan but he seems all right, standing head and shoulders over the parapet. Pig has his head showing and I boot him.

'Fritz'll have a Parapet Joe over there — machine-gunner who slices his bullets on the trenchline. Would you like a bullet in the head or the chest?'

He gets the message and straightens. You may survive a chest or shoulder wound, not a bullet in the head. A smashed shoulder is a ticket home and nobody can call that self-inflicted.

I go to a trench periscope but there's nothing to see. Evening shadows break the ground in dark lines and there are coils of wire like huge spiked cobwebs. Even so, I look at it carefully because this will be my hunting ground. I have to know it, the way a tiger knows the jungle.

Like the tiger, I will hunt at night.

The first couple of days go quietly. The Huns want that, for us to settle in and relax. Then, the second night, there are shots down the line and flares go up. A Hun patrol has snatched an A Company sentry, shortly after midnight.

By morning they will know who we are, maybe our strength. They're good at asking questions.

Breakfast that third morning is the same as always. Bully beef out of a can, something called 'Tickler's jam' on the tooth-breaking army biscuits. I bet Tickler's making a fortune. I can already feel a tiny prickling under my arms, on my body. Lice are like Huns — lose no time in making their presence felt, and they're just as difficult to get rid of.

I shave out of a tin cup and the cold dawn cuts at my raw cheeks. Go out, kick the morning watch awake. Brasso tells me to get stuffed but he'd better not mean it. I don't play favourites.

Sergeant McKinnon appears with Rowlands. McKinnon is better now, realising he needs a few blokes like me. Rowlands is puffy-eyed from sleep, cheeks as raw as mine, and jokes about this place not being the Ritz — whatever that is.

Creel, unshaven, pushes past, muttering about liaison with HQ. He's off down the communication sap. Odds on we won't see him again all day.

The morning hate session comes next and we huddle under the parapet as the yellow smoke drifts around us and sandbags collapse. Our own guns reply and a few thousand quids worth of shells are fired before it dies down.

Then comes a loud voice. 'Hello, En-Zed soldier. You get boot from Gallipoli. Now you come here and get boot too, *ja*?'

The voice has a heavy German accent. The

28

words ring out of the morning. 'You fight for fat Empire merchant and banker. Come over, we will give you warm welcome.'

'Warm' is 'varm'. A few hoots and boos, our men more interested in sleep than listening to this crap. I'm getting the pricker though. Booted out of Gallipoli? *All right, sausage-eaters. Let's see!*

'Periscope, Brasso,' I mutter.

'They've got a megaphone or loudspeaker out in no-man's land,' says Rowlands. 'Must be on wire from their trenches.'

Hell, Mr Rowlands, you mean like the Turks at Gallipoli? Only when they tried to speak English, we were too busy laughing to listen. Oh, I forgot, Mr Rowlands, you weren't in the trenches there, were you? So I pretend not to hear Rowlands and he takes the hint and shuts up. Another sign of a good officer.

He has the periscope just above the sandbags because Huns love to shoot at them. Holds it while I look through. Yeah, there it is. A coil of rusting wire and some bodies, swollen and recent. One with an arm hooked over and in the shadow below, a round blackness. I nod to Brasso, we've done this before — with human targets.

'Seventy yards,' he says.

The French have this metric thing, kilometres, too damn confusing for me. I adjust the sights on my Lee Enfield and nod to Brasso.

'Careful, corp,' murmurs Rowlands, 'they may be expecting this.'

He's green but learning fast. Of course they are bloody expecting it, Mr Rowlands, sharpshooters sighting on our trenchline right now — waiting for some new boy to show himself. That's why they made the megaphone just visible.

But we know how to play that game.

'Fernleaf,' says the Hun voice, getting some chuckles because he says it 'Vernsleeves'. 'Britain wants your blood. Their soldiers take your women.'

'They can have my missus,' mutters Brasso.

'My mother-in-law,' murmurs Rowlands.

'Vernsleeves, come over, get good welcome, money, all the *schnapps* you can drink. More money if you bring your rifle. We gif hand of friendship.'

'Ready,' whispers Brasso.

'Vernsleeves, we tell you how to come over. Listen —'

I'm crouched on the firing step, *up*, a moment to steady myself and shoot. Duck over the flat crack of the rifle, so familiar. Brasso looks again.

'Maybe a foot to the right.'

'Not such a good shot there,' blares the loudspeaker. 'You haf to do better —'

I'm up again, another snapshot. The loudspeaker spins out, I should duck. *I'll show them* — work the bolt, fire again, duck very fast as the loudspeaker shatters. Bullets thud into the sandbags, I swear the first scrapes the top of my helmet.

'Nearly copped it, you bloody show-off,' grins Brasso.

We can hear other loudspeakers up and down the line. The Huns must have gone to a lot of trouble last night. I eject an empty cartridge and it tinkles on the firing step. I reach in my pocket, press my thumb over the sharp point of my Turkish bullet.

This bullet is special. From a Turkish sniper's rifle, he'd intended to use it on me. It had a word scratched on the brass casing that I had translated. *Faith*. I do no sniping without that bullet, it's lucky for me.

'Nice work, corporal,' says Rowlands warmly.

'Worth a bottle of rum in Gallipoli, sir,' says Brasso cheerfully.

'I'll remember that if we're ever back there,' grins Rowlands, just as cheerfully.

But — surprise — we do get a bottle of plonk that evening. The thin stuff you can drink all day, but better than nothing. And so ends my first shoot.

It's time the Huns learned Corporal Moran was here.

Eileen

WE WERE TWELVE weeks at Shoreditch and I met her at some patriotic rally. We 'walked out' together and there was this one time when we took shelter under a railway bridge from rain. And sort of stayed there an hour or two. Then, just before we sail, she sends a note for me. I go around to the big house where she works. Back door of course, tradesmen and soldiers.

'I've missed, Jacko. All the signs. I am going to have one.'

'Hell. Well, we'll just have to get married then.'

'Do you want to marry me?'

'Suppose so. Sure. I don't mind.'

'Because there are ways of not having to — get married.'

'What d'you mean, Eileen?'

'You know ... a 'bortion. There's this chemist in High Street but he only deals with gents. Not if a woman asks him, it's gotta come from the man.'

'I'm not a gent, Eileen, I'm a bloody solider. More like he won't. He don't know me.'

'Well, there's a woman in Drivers Alley, kind of midwife. She does it if the girl asks.'

'You sure about this?'

'Jacko, I'm below-stairs. You know the score. Nobody'd give me a job with a bastard kid. I'd have to go on the game.'

'It wouldn't be a bastard if we got married —'

'Jacko, I like you, but I'm in a good house. No married servants, let alone kids. I won't get another chance like this. I can make lady's maid. That's eight bob a week and perks. I want that, Jacko. I want better.'

'Geez. How much then?'

'Fiver.'

'Five quid! All right, all right, chrissake, stop blubbing —'

'Thanks, Jacko. Ta, ever so.'

'Will I see you again?'

'Best not. Might cost another fiver.'

'You sure this thing's safe?'

'Oh yes, lots of girls have it. Better go now, Jacko, it's a fair hike over there and I'm on me half day.'

'Here, go on, take a cab.'

'Never, I'll take the bus. Ta, Jacko, really ta. Good luck. Hey, maybe they'll make you an officer.'

'Some chance. Bye, Eileen.'

I told Brasso about it on the Channel ship. He laughed, oldest trick in the book; she'll have spun that yarn to all her boyfriends.

I did write to Eileen and she never answered.

I never saw her again.

Trenchline is routine most of the time — a bloody awful routine and very different from Gallipoli. In the forward trenches, we rest all day — try to sleep. There's always a Hun shell or two dropping, 'Moaning Minnie', 'Dustbins', 'Coal Boxes', or even mortar rounds — 'Pineapples'. We spend our nights on patrol or sentry-go, or repairing damage, always something to do.

Eight days in the front line, then eight in the second line. Then base lines and a change of routine. We get to spend the day working and the night trying to sleep. Better food, even showers and delousing.

We're in Armentières, same as the song but no mademoiselles. It's supposed to be a quiet part of the lines, but the mud and bloody rats, bully beef, lice and army hardtack are the same. And staying alive when the Huns want us dead.

Well, so did the Turks and I survived them. Rumour says the Huns will try a 'big push' soon and then — the old Flanders lags tell us — we'll find out what a real war is all about, not sunbathing at Anzac Cove.

I've never got anything for when the mailsack comes around. Just that once to Eileen. Kate and Ellen left home about when I did. Only other blokes I know are right here — or dead. If I get shot, nobody will give a damn. So what the hell, talk of a Hun offensive doesn't worry me. I'm in the mood for a good fight.

'Intelligence reports say the Huns are up to a fair bit on our line,' says Creel. Just a candle going in his dugout, he looks puffy and pale; place reeks of alcohol. 'Digging new saps, a lot of movement. Might be a local offensive so HQ want a prisoner. Six-man patrol, Moran, you've done this before.' He smiles.

'Yes, sir.'

A 'snatch' — dirty risky job. Just what Creel would land me with. McKinnon and Rowlands are jammed in the dugout with me. McKinnon makes to speak and doesn't. Rowlands does.

'Sir, that's a job for a lieutenant, not a corporal, surely? My job, sir.'

Creel's smile goes, but Rowlands is right and Creel lives by the rule-book. So he nods, 'Well, shows the right spirit, lieutenant. Of course you'll be taking Moran along.'

Rowlands nods. *Yes, of course, thanks for nothing!* I snap to attention, give that grin that Creel hates.

'Like old times, sir. Pity you're not coming with us.'

There were no 'old times' at Gallipoli and Creel knows it. He avoided patrols like he avoided everything. I get a look. My grin and snappy salute say, '*Sod you, pig,*' and I exit.

'Thanks, corp,' says Rowlands outside, *as if I had a choice*. He hesitates, no officer likes admitting other-ranks know more. 'Ah … you've had more experience of this …'

'Go out at midnight, sir. Lay a while, get 'em at dawn when they're half-asleep.'

'Right. Midnight.'

'Black up, sir. Number Two Forward Observation, midnight?'

'Black up, Number Two,' he repeats and heads for his dugout.

I pick my men. Brasso of course and Duncan. He pleads a gut-ache, so it's Pig, Bingham and Apple-yard. The last two are fast learners and Pig has muscle. I tell them what's wanted, to get food and rest.

My first night patrol. It's like old times. And like old times, that sick-stomach feeling and the cold sweat. But I do now want to come through this and anything else Flanders can chuck at me. If for no other reason, because of unfinished business with Rupert Maggot Creel.

MIDNIGHT. NUMBER Two Post. I check equipment, everyone blacked, armed for trench fighting. Rifles and bayonets just get in the way. I have a short club, studded with horseshoe nails. Pig and Connor have hatchets and Brasso has got his little trenching spade, the edge filed to razor sharpness. Rowlands turns up in trenchcoat, complete with grenades on the belt, revolver attached to a lanyard around his neck. He looks like one of those ads for Army and Navy stores; nervous as hell but so's everyone and they should be.

Nervous people stay alert and this will be no fun at all.

Creel actually comes up, a handshake with Rowlands. Signals already arranged, different-coloured flares, for time, covering fire, etc. Forward sentry asks about password.

'Yellow rabbit,' I say. Very easy to remember and I don't look at Creel.

Then we go out into the blackness, stink and gut-wrenching tension of no-man's land. The moon will be up soon, I want to be well into it by then.

The Tommies left maps and notes. Not technical stuff, but written by blokes like me, who used every hump and crater; even if that meant crawling over dead bodies alive with maggots. I crawl, the others behind, just touching. Once I hear a muffled retching sound and whisper savagely for silence. The Huns have their own listening patrols out.

Wire scrapes us like razor fingernails. Once I put my hand on something cold and clammy. A man's face, long dead. I feel ahead for the little points of buried mines or tripwires maybe rigged last night when they set up the loudspeakers. The night around me, like being wrapped in a thick black stinking blanket.

Must be ten times worse for the others behind.

Odd thoughts as I inch forward, Rowlands' hands touching my boots as he follows. My old man, Eileen. The plain wooden box they put Mum in. Gallipoli memories, thick and dark as the blanket. *A fiver. Geez, Eileen must have laughed!*

The moon is coming out. I belly through an icy puddle and hiss for everyone to stop. Rowlands crawls up beside me. His nice new raincoat is a stinking mess now.

'Where are we?' he whispers.

'German forward post about twenty yards ahead,' I whisper back, hoping like hell I'm right. Cup my hand, a brief torch-blink: 0100. We've been crawling in this stinking black muck for an hour. If I have followed the map then the German observation post is ahead.

Nothing to do now but wait, three hours to first light, so a bloody long wait. They'll have to lie in the cold mud without moving and like it. Or they'll die under a hail of Jerry hand-bombs. There are no second chances on a patrol like this.

'You'll get your mucking head shot off.'

Giving my dad money. Hell, should've called his bluff, he was glad to be shot of me, I was too big to hit any more. I bet he went on an almighty bender. And laughed — like Eileen.

Gallipoli was the first good thing that happened to me. I was a fighter so I was valued. I was cow-cakes crude but I was somebody. A fancy education meant nothing, gutter-skills meant everything. Pinching fruit off barrows, taking a drunk's watch, scrapping when another gang muscled in on our street. The cops never got me and nor did the Turks.

Now it's Flanders, maybe years of it. Some rifle-fire and mortars, the stutter of a machine-gun. Our side returns the fire, because keeping quiet will alert the Huns.

A German signal flare rises and bursts, dazzling yellow. Flares are the only splash of colour in no-man's land and deadly, if that lovely colour lights you up. A flare from our line, fired at an angle so as not to show us. It burns green into red, to remind us it is four a.m.

Time to go.

I am aching cold and frozen numb. My face seems glued to the black muck, a popping sound under my cheek as I look around and whisper.

'Ready, sir?'

Not waiting, the painful business of inching forward again. The German post outlined in very pale dawnlight. Now, from it, we can hear noise.

A mutter of voices, a clink as something is poured. Noise is good because silence would mean they were waiting. Grasping my baton, thinking of the first Turk skull I cracked with it — as he tried to gut me with his bayonet. Rowlands whispers back, very tense.

'Ready.'

'You'll get your mucking head shot off!'

Get control! Forget everything but this. Nod because Rowlands can see that in the growing light. The others behind him, humped shadows. The glint of

Brasso's trench-spade, good to know he's there, forget about Duncan's sudden gut ache.

And realising I must move first. Getting up, wincing as the utter cold strikes through, on my feet and crouched low. I run the last few yards in moments, the others behind me.

They will hear us but too late. Over the sandbags and jumping down. White faces upturned, eyes wide, mouths open. A mug of coffee spilled, grabbing weapons. Down comes my baton on a helmeted head. Storming through the post, kicking, whacking out with the baton. The flat crack of Rowlands' Webley — *should have told him not to shoot!*

German bodies pushed against me. I'm rolling in the trench muck with a Hun, his eyes slitted. He's lost his rifle, grabbing for his bayonet. His eyes roll up white as Brasso's spade hits the back of his neck. His breath stinks of onions as he death-rattles.

Kicking free and scrambling up, looking around. Shouts now, as the Huns down-trench get a response together. Eight in this post, dead or wounded. Pig, his chest heaving, puts a foot on a body to wrench his hatchet free. Rowlands clicks his empty revolver and fumbles in his pocket for bullets.

'Leave that, sir!' Bullets won't stop Hun grenades. 'Get that one!'

'That one' being a young soldier, blood down one side of his face. The first one I hit. Pig and Appleyard grab him, pull him over the tumbled sandbags. Bingham, Brasso, me and Rowlands, a stick-bomb comes sailing towards us. Falls in the post, the explosion kills their own men.

Back now and no more crawling, fast as we can. Rowlands still thinking, firing his flare pistol into the dawn sky. Green, weeping bright tears, meaning we are on our way home, *so covering fire*!

It comes. Mortars, machine-guns and rifle-fire, sparking like the gas-lights of a theatre. And behind us, the Hun trenchlines spit yellow and send that whack-hum of bullets around us.

We are running low, bundling the Jerry along. Bingham throws up his arms and pitches forward. Bullet-holes in his back, face-down in the mud, *dead — leave him*! We run on, splashing water, through the sleeting bullets. The Ob. Post ahead — what was that oh-so-clever password? Creel will laugh if —

'Yellow rabbit!'

And we are across, knocking aside a Lewis gun and the cursing gunner. Down in a heap, boots kicking. Brasso's damn spade nearly gabbing my face. Pig yelling, come and see the Hun. I shout 'shut up' so loud I swear the firing dies for a moment.

Sergeant McKinnon is waiting at the command post. Creel has gone to HQ, leaving orders for the prisoner to be sent on. A hell of a racket still and by candlelight, we get a look at our snatch.

He's thickset, black hair cut very short, maybe against lice. Uniform thick with mud but good cloth so hasn't been in the trenches long. Brasso's eyeing his boots, he won't keep those long. Or his watch and signet-ring. He's fearful, tight-lipped — he'll have been told we kill prisoners after torturing them.

'All right, get him out,' says Rowlands.

Brasso and Pig bundle him out. Rowlands' batman hands us mugs of hot sweet tea, tastes better than rum right now. Rowlands sips his tea, adds more sugar.

'You don't like Captain Creel, do you?'

There's different ways to answer an officer. No answer sometimes, or the beloved dumb insolence. I look at the sandbag walls, the pinned cut-out of George the Fifth, another of a British Bulldog with tin helmet. That tells Rowlands better than words.

'All right, corp. Well done. Get some sleep.'

He can read what he likes into my silence. I give him a snappy salute and exit. He can read what he likes into that, too.

Outside, a cool fresh breeze. Flares criss-cross the sky like fireworks — Mum took us to those when King George was crowned, when I was thirteen.

The shooting is dying down, the Huns know they've lost their man. We have a prisoner and I have not lost my hunting skills. I have what it takes to be a sniper. A full dawn now, outlining the sandbags in pink.

I am blooded and feel good; that cutting thrill goes through me. I have done my job well, I'm still bloody good at what I do. That matters, that's important here.

Now to use my skills doing what I am good at. Put away those thoughts of my father, even of Eileen's cheap trick — they'll get me killed. Hope Brasso returns soon, bet he found a bottle in that Hun post. And too bad about Bingham, Rowlands will have to write a letter.

I put Bingham from my mind too. I'm thinking about a Hun, one who's still over there. And with a strange bloody nickname for someone alive and well.

Dead Willi.

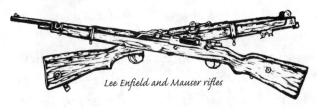

Lee Enfield and Mauser rifles

ABOUT A WEEK after we arrive, the Hun lays down a box barrage. That's when they zero all their artillery into one sector — ours, this time.

It's like a storm, all night and day. This storm howls and howls and thunders non-stop, full of flying lead. I'm in a shelter with Brasso and Duncan. Duncan is on his bed, hands clasped over his head. Brasso tries to play patience but the cards jump up and down and he gives up in disgust. I'm watching Duncan. He was going like this at Gallipoli. Shell-fire does that to some blokes. And then his gut-wound. He should never have been sent back. The rain starts again and the Hun gunners stop. Maybe they were getting wet.

Sergeant McKinnon is yelling for trench-parties to repair the damage. Brasso slips his cards back into a silver case, won it off an Aussie at blackjack. Duncan just sits there, white-faced and hands shaking too much to hold a spade. Brasso and me eyeline and leave Duncan where he is. Poor bugger.

The trench is a mess. One dugout collapsed, two guys buried but we get them out in time. Sandbags collapsed and rats everywhere. Big ones, on their backs, concussed by the shelling. Some of us staggering, white and sick, feeling as bad as the rats.

A runner, Ericson, picks up one by its tail, whirls it around and throws it into no-man's land. Laughs, picks up another and straightens. But he's by a collapsed section of parapet. Me and Brasso shout a warning — too late.

Crack! Ericson pitches back, a neat dark hole in his forehead. He gargles, twitches, he's gone. The gunshot, the bullet-wound, are a bloody trademark.

Dead Willi.

Once a day or two, a batch of clean socks come around. We all grab a couple, never mind if they don't match; at least they're clean and dry. Wet socks bring on trench-foot and (as Brasso explains) the generals want us fit and healthy to be shot at.

Pig is grumbling at the latest order. We (Wellington battalion) wear the peaked 'lemon-squeezer' hats — when we're not wearing tin hats. Seems now the whole New Zealand Army will wear them.

Pig doesn't want to look like just another soldier. Brasso says Pig could never look like anything other than what he is. Pig (thinking it's a compliment) says we should have a different hat, like those slouch ones with the side turned up.

A moment of silence. 'And look like *Aussies*?' says Brasso.

Pig goes under a hail of boots.

'Getting at the Hun are we, lads?'

We? Lads?

Brasso, Pig and me are up at a forward post. Brasso has a trench periscope, we're trying to spot Dead Willi and keeping our heads well down. Half a mile of no-man's land between us and the Huns — lots of hiding places.

So the bloke takes us by surprise. Civvy flannels and a bloody sports jacket! He's young, thin, spectacles, named Ambrose Trantor, journalist for *Illustrated Weekly News*. Tells us chronic asthma and bad eyesight kept him out of the army — quickly, like he's said it to every soldier he meets.

'If I look over the parapet, will I see a Hun?'

'There's a Hun called Willi hoping like hell you'll try,' says Brasso.

Hot day, the mud black and stinking. Trantor's brought sandwiches up — real bread and real slices of ham — and shares them around. Of course the flies home in and he looks with dismay. 'What d'you do about the flies?'

'Nice and fat, taste better than the Gallipoli ones, eh, corp?' says Pig.

'Get used to them.' Brasso sticks his sandwich, flies and all, into his mouth. He winks at me, my turn.

'Bodies are worse,' I say. 'They swell up in the heat, you're on patrol, stick your foot in one and it explodes like a huge fart. Stinks awful, and the Huns hear it, next thing there's pineapples coming down like it's Christmas.'

'Look at this,' says Pig, reaching under his armpit to bring out a handful of lice. 'Little buggers breed on us.'

'Rats,' says Brasso, 'all over the trench, eat your toes off if you give them a chance. Bloke I know, lost his nose.'

'Do you want that sandwich, mate?' asks Pig.

Trantor doesn't. In fact, he has to be getting on but wants us to know what heroes we are. He scrambles off, bent double, hand over his mouth. Pig gets the sandwich.

We read the article a few weeks later. About bullets flying thickly overhead, and how our bronzed warriors man the firing step, fearlessly returning the fire. Nothing about flies or bodies or rats. It reads like a different war. An illustration showing clean-shaven infantry in neat uniforms, attacking the cowardly pig-faced Huns who are running or surrendering.

Most of the scribblers never get past Base HQ and a good lunch. If they get to the Front, they never stay long; especially if they have to dodge a cowardly Hun's bullet.

With the article is a photo of the New Zealand graves at Armentières. Seems like we get a nice stone marker with a fernleaf on it; and our name.

AND SERGEANT McKinnon's not half bad, now he's realised Creel is a complete no-hoper. He was there for Ericson's funeral, says there are whole rows of fresh-dug graves; the sign of a new battle coming. Until then, they'll have to fill up slowly. Shell-fire, trench raids — and other ways.

There was this bloke in A company whose wife wrote she was having someone else's baby. Takes off his boot, puts rifle in his mouth, and presses the trigger with his big toe. Stupid says Brasso, all he had to do was stick his head over the parapet. Because there's a Hun out there, always waiting for blokes like him.

Dead Willi.

DEAD WILLI is a Hun sniper who everyone on this sector gets to know quickly. The battalion before us lost sixteen men, mostly officers. His nickname was Dead-shot Willi, shortened now to 'Dead Willi' because if he sees you, you're dead.

His trademark is the single head-shot and this part of the lines is his personal hunting ground. Hun prisoners talk about him and Willi spends more time in no-man's land than his own trenches. Most men have never seen him — he moves like a shadow, like a ghost. And he's very good at what he does.

We find that out bloody quick.

A Company had a lot of new blokes, but they had four less at the end of the first week, including a lieutenant. B Company sends out a ten-man patrol, only six get back; the sergeant and lieutenant not among them. Nobody saw Dead Willi.

C Company had Bert Spinner, nearly as damn good as me. He goes out one night to hunt Dead Willi. Early next morning they hear a single shot. It doesn't come from Spinner's Enfield. The next patrol finds him — and loses two men doing it.

Now it's the turn of B Company. Snipers are like dogs pissing on a lamp-post. They have to leave their mark everywhere. Another new boy, McCready, on night watch. He forgets why three on a match is un-lucky. Lights for his mates, takes a moment longer to light his own pipe. That moment is all Dead Willi needs.

'WE'LL HAVE TO do something about that bugger,' says Brasso.

We? I give him a long hard look and get a very innocent one back. Rowlands appears and Brasso disappears. He uses the trench periscope for a look around no-man's land. 'Corporal, you know about this kind of work. Where's he likely to be?'

Where? Any bloody place, snipers don't hang out flags. Maybe he's under a tree-stump or dug in the side of a shell-crater. I shot one Turk who used a rotting corpse for cover. Maybe there are several rat-holes, all booby-trapped when not in use.

Rowlands listens, still using the periscope. I'm about to tell him it's not wise to flash that, when Dead Willi says it better. A crack and tinkle, Rowlands curses as the periscope is jerked from his hands.

'Willi's just keeping his hand in, sir.'

I'm thinking about that crack though. I know the 'Toc' noise a Mauser rifle makes — I've heard it enough times, and that's not one. More likely a new custom-made job, telescopic sights, shoots at one mile; a soft-nosed bullet that kills anywhere it hits. A gun like that is well worth having.

Rowlands brushes broken glass off his jacket. 'Getting Willi,' he says slowly, 'will be a job for a volunteer.'

I nearly say take out an ad in *The Times*. I want to get Willi but don't like being pushed into it. And even thinking that, I nod to him. I was kingpin at

Gallipoli and kingpins have to keep proving it. Plus I can feel the old excitement coming back. The Poms before us, the Canadians before them, had some crack shots and they couldn't get Dead Willi.

Now it's the turn of Jacko Moran.

I wait another night because I want Willi to get restless for another victim. Snipers do that. I clean my Enfield. I'll travel light with a couple of spare magazines, some crackers, a trench-knife and a canteen. One bullet is all it takes — and all the chance I'll get.

'A FIVER SAYS you don't make it.'

That's Brasso's way of saying good luck and take care. Duncan just smiles and we handshake. I black up, pull the blanket and scatter Brasso's solitaire game. His curse follows me out.

Up by the forward post, Rowlands is waiting. 'You don't have to do this,' he says.

Yes, Mr Rowlands, I bloody well do. The buzz has gone up the line about Jacko Moran so there's no backing down. And that feeling is back, like nothing you can describe. Like cold fire or needles prickling all over my skin.

I do have a chance. Willi's had it his own way for a long time. Maybe it's becoming a routine, maybe he's getting careless. Most of his shots come from the middle of no-man's land. There were farms here once, the houses now smashed to their foundations. Any number of good rat-holes in the ruins.

Time to go. Rowlands mutters good luck, puts out his hand for me to shake. I pretend not to see it, don't answer. I'm focused on Willi, not Rowlands. I go through the wire into darkness, press the outline of the Turk bullet in my pocket. *Faith!*

A lot of bodies because the Poms tried a push before we came. The usual slaughter and no truce day yet to bury the dead. No point either, when the shell-fire just digs them up again. And it's bloody cold.

I'm not looking for Willi tonight. I want to find a hide of my own and I have one spotted. An uprooted tree-stump, the roots sticking in the air. It's shell-blasted and the soil is soft. I dig quietly with my trench-knife and snuggle in, throwing as much dirt over me as I can. Exposing a skeleton hand as I do.

And I wait.

It's bloody uncomfortable. The rifle is jammed beside me, the tree-roots spread along the front, with a few little gaps for me to keep watch through. My legs are cramped and my back aches, but I huddle tight. The smaller the hole the better.

The sun comes up and I don't move. Sweat begins to drip down my face and prickle my eyes and a pain starts in my leg. I don't move — the pain's better than a bullet in the head — because Willi is around. I can smell him. Maybe he can smell me too. It's like a thickening in the air, a sense of danger. Mid-morning and the shells are whistling over — Minnies, by the sound of them. There's some small-arms racket too because our men are under orders to behave normally. Holding their fire would be like sending Willi a telegram.

I can see the smashed ruins of the farmhouse now. It's little more than a line of tumbled stonework. The foundation lines of a drystone wall, a shattered wagon-wheel among the stones.

Was there a cellar in that house? Maybe, but our patrols and theirs have crawled over it a dozen times without seeing one. Artillery must have the range to a yard. No, he'd avoid the house.

So wait.

You wouldn't think it could get so quiet in no-man's land. So quiet I can hear my heart beating. I don't dare even glance at my watch — look away and I might miss something. The sun's high and it's time that lazy bugger Brasso remembers what to do.

He'll be lifting the tip of a helmet on his bayonet, just a little, like someone ducking carelessly along the trench. Not too obvious, because Dead Willi knows all the tricks. Just enough to get his interest, tempt him; after all, we're green troops, those 'Vernsleeves' who got booted out of Gallipoli.

Ready when you are, Willi.

Soon Brasso will stop and go back to his card

game for half an hour. They're repairing the parapet today, extending a sap to the rear. So lots of activity, lots of interest for Willi. Brasso will start again in half an hour.

No score yesterday, Willi. *Think of your reputation!*

Duncan seems OK but I know the signs. Will he break? The Poms have shot a lot of their men for that, but most are just blokes who've had too much. Lack of moral fibre is what the bloody brass say, but you don't have to be a coward to break. Forget about Duncan — *concentrate!*

Come on, Willi, the Kaiser'll give you a medal. The Iron Cross, Willi, that'll get the *frauleins* in a flutter. 'Course, I'd like to give you a cross too, Willi. A little wooden one, with R.I.P. on it.

Crack!

Near the ruined farmhouse! I'm looking, scanning, not moving — that will kill me. No smoke, but did I see a tiny wobble of movement? Oh, you cunning bloody Hun, I think I've got you spotted!

But spotting Willi and getting him are two different things. He'll be snuggled back down now in his nice little hole. I have to go to him and not in broad daylight. Tonight.

And he's very smart. I told Brasso to keep up the helmet-bobbing but Willi's too smart a fish to bite twice. He may even eat something and rest; and he'll sleep with one eye open. But I do have to get closer.

Tonight.

WHEN IT'S very black and cold, I ease out from under the stump. I belly forward in the frozen mud and bits of wire, sharp edges of bone or shell-fragments cut at me; my uniform'll be in tatters by morning. A frost tonight, the wind cutting like icy razors. I used to hate the hot dry winds of Gallipoli.

Willi, I'm coming for you.

Funny thought as I crawl forward. I don't know Willi any more than those Turks. But I sniped at them and on truce days, we traded and smiled. I'm sweating, funny how that never seems to freeze — Lord, it's cold.

A shell-crater ahead like the black bulk of a crouching animal. Over the humped rim and inside. I know this crater, broken at one end by another shell. That's my route to the farm ruins, but Willi will have it spotted. And targeted. He might even sense that I'm here by now and be waiting.

My knee scrapes painfully on an empty tin. Thin ice crackles, sounding much too loud, and I pause long moments. I move again and almost hook a shattered rusty helmet with my boot, just save it from clattering down. Around me, it's dark. Some flares spotting the dark sky red. The long burr-burr of the Vickers. They always sound so different from the Spandaus.

The farmhouse ruins are ahead in the darkness. But I have been moving and Willi has the smarts of a wolf. So I huddle to the frozen ground, push my rifle ahead into position and wait. The dawn must come again, enough light to see and to shoot.

Or be shot.

The sky lightens. Rainwater in frozen slippery patches, be *so* careful, the crack of breaking ice will kill me. I inch a little closer, a big shell-hole this; made by a dustbin at least. Head down, I can't even let a cloud of frosty breath be seen.

Dawn. The thick frozen muck builds on my face, my frozen fingers digging in the mud as I inch closer. Ice breaks like a thousand windows shattering. *Freeze!*

More light and I'm aware of something glassy, not quite human, beside me. A bloated face, eyeballs staring, all covered with thin ice. Just the head itself, teeth bared as though all this is a mad joke. Ha, ha, Willi's going to get you.

You'll get your mucking head shot off!

Willi knows I'm here, he must. I ease off my helmet and prop it on my trench knife. I have to flush him out but light is on his side and so is ground. He can wait but I'm picking he wants me because this is *his* ground and trespassers will be shot.

I raise the helmet. Will he be fooled? Think some clumsy Vernleeve is out there? Crack!

Hell, that was quick! The helmet spins away but I'm watching through something black and splintered that was once human ribs. A *movement*, near those stones and broken cartwheel. It wobbled again, a rifle-barrel between the spokes, drawn from sight.

Got you, Willi.

But I've got to flush him out, make him shoot again. This duel's like poker, bluff and double-bluff. He won't be fooled by a helmet again ... maybe ... the thought comes to me ... he can be fooled by a bullet. But first I have to do something horrible.

Horrible, it will turn my stomach. But it's been done before, that little Gurkha at Anzac Cove; grinning like a toothpaste ad, telling me how to flush that Turk sniper.

Tense, push the rifle forward. This has to be the quickest of snap-shots. Crack! The wheel jerks, splinters fly and I duck. No answering bullet, but I wasn't expecting one. He will wait for a target and this time, be very bloody careful.

Head down, I push the trench-knife into the frozen black mud beside me. The thin ice crackles but I want him to hear me now and be waiting. My knife scrapes over a neckbone and I lever out that grinning head, like cutting a rotten cabbage from the ground.

Somebody's head, British or German, filthy as hell but still nearly human. I stick it on my trench-knife. Willi got my helmet — he won't be fooled like that again. Sure, horrible, I don't even look at the scraggly thing, swollen like a football. There are no rules and, with any luck, the head belonged to a staff officer.

I work the bolt on my rifle and push it out again, holding it in place with one hand. The head is stuck on my trench-knife and I raise it slowly with the other hand. Very slowly, the stupid Vernleeve wants to see if he hit anything. Very tense, there will be this one moment —

Crack! — the awful football head shatters. Both hands on the rifle, sight and fire with eyeblinking speed, work the bolt and fire again. The wheel bucks, more splinters fly. Do I hear a cry or was it stones clattering?

They'll have heard this at our trenches. So will the Germans. But I can't move yet, peep between those blackened bones, hand cupped over my steaming breath. Something white between the spokes, something else long and teetering. The white thing is a hand, the long thing is a rifle. It overbalances and falls away from the spoke.

Could be a trick. I snapshot again and the hand falls back in. Sunlight glints on the telescopic sights of the rifle, long-barrelled and sleek deadly lines. I want it and I need to move fast. And I need to know Willi is dead.

So I crawl forward, my rifle ahead, alert for movement He could just be wounded, have a pistol. I crawl fast, it's dangerous, even stupid, because the Germans will send out a patrol to help their top man. I belly over the stonework of the old wall and around to the cartwheel. As I figured, it's open at the back.

He is there, lying on his belly, one hand outflung. Duckboards there and sandbags, a nice snug rathole. He could be faking, could have a bomb or a Luger; rifle in one hand, I grab his foot and pull him out.

One wound, went in at the base of his throat, through the body. Blood everywhere, but his eyes flicker. He's very short and thin, sharp-faced with pitted cheeks. Mousy hair cut very short, looks ordinary as hell. He's looking at me, trying to speak, one hand going weakly to his tunic pocket.

'I don't speak mucking German,' I whisper.

Then his hand flops, his painful eyes go blank. Dead Willi is dead. *It was you or me, Willi, fair fight!*

A clatter in the distance, a growling voice. German patrol coming. I pull the papers from Willi's pocket, his watch too. Binoculars, ammunition clips — *get moving!*

I scramble over the wheel, grab the rifle and run back to the crater. More noise and voices as I do, if they don't mind talking, then they're mob handed, lots of them. Back at the crater, I hear the first 'Toc' of Mauser rifles.

I fling myself down. There's an angry shout — they've found Willi. And something angry builds in me. I've been crawling in a frozen black stink, used a human head as a target. I've watched a skinny kid die because I wanted to be tops. *OK, you are tops. Start behaving like it!*

So I turn, working the bolt on my Enfield. Yes, the Hun patrol spread out, trying to work around. Careless with it, think I am on the run. Crack! The first man spins around, his helmet falling off. Crack! A second man staggers at the stonework. Work the bolt, squeeze the trigger — a third man collides with the second and both fall.

Mortars are coming from our side now, soon from theirs. A hate session will start, so I yell while I still can.

'Get this, you mucking sausage-eaters! I got your boy and his bloody rifle. I'm kingpin now, me, Jacko Moran! You muckers come into my ground and you'll never leave!'

More bullets and now the distant 'crump' of German mortars. Their pineapples will be coming over so I get out, quickly. Down an old collapsed sap line, shouting the password as I take a header into the post. Roll over, my rifles clattering, not even a bloody challenge from the sentry, what the hell —

It's Brasso, grinning down at me. I learn later he was there all last night. Puts out his hand, pulls me up.

'You owe me a fiver, Brasso.'

ROWLANDS IS HAVING breakfast in his dugout. He gives me a mug of coffee and I suddenly realise how hungry I am. Burr-burr of the Vickers outside as he examines the rifle.

'Mannlicher, 8mm, damn fine weapon. Adjustable telescopic sights, side-bore mounting. They don't just hand these things out, Dead Willi must have been good.'

He was good. Two chances at me, both times should've killed. But don't even think about souveniring the rifle, Mr Rowlands. I firmly take it back and he smiles. 'But not good enough, eh Moran?'

'I got him sir, so that makes me better.'

Rowlands raises his eyebrows. 'Self-advertisement is no recommendation, corporal. And that's one expensive rifle. The Huns will want it back.'

'They know where to find it, sir'

'Oh yes. Jacko Moran is kingpin?'

It does sound a bit silly now. 'You heard that, sir?'

'I should think all Flanders did.'

I hand him the papers I took from Willi's pocket. Not the watch. He nods. 'Bloody well done, corporal. Now get some food and rest. And —'

'Sir?'

'Don't be in too much of a hurry to prove yourself, or you'll end up like Erlich Krebs.'

'Who?'

'Dead Willi. That was his name.'

'Sir.'

I go back to hardtack, bully-beef and jam. About a gallon of hot tea, laced with rum. I let Duncan and Brasso look at the Mannlicher, just once. After this, nobody touches it but me.

I'm bone-tired but somehow not sleepy. That thrill is still pumping through me. I go out into the trenchline, muddy from head to foot, my uniform in tatters. A couple of new boys gape at me, they all heard that shout in no-man's land. I took risks I didn't have to and killed a man I did not know. Now the Huns will have me targeted. All crazy, but I feel good. I beat Willi.

I remember something. The pitting on his cheeks, lots of kids had it where I lived. An army doctor said it was bad food and not enough of it. So Willi was a slum kid, like me? A street rat using his skills, till he met another street rat.

And one other thing. In the rifle butt, a small compartment for cleaning gear … and a photo. A dark-haired girl, shy smile, in a flowered dress, sitting on a chair. On the back of the photo, a name. Trudi.

Wife, girlfriend, even sister? Only whatshisname — Crabs, Crebs — knows who, and he is past asking. I drop it in a puddle and put my boot on it.

He's past wanting it.

Mannlicher

ARMENTIÈRES WAS supposed to be a 'quiet' part of the lines where new troops could be safely 'blooded'.

That's an expression the generals love. Means we get used to bleeding and dying, says Brasso.

Our trenchline became suddenly unsafe as the British launched a new offensive at the Somme. Their 'New Army' attacked the Germans, a head-on assault against machine-guns. We'd tried that in Gallipoli under some of the same generals, with the same result. The British lose sixty thousand men in a few hours.

That's about one-fifth the population of New Zealand. Over the next weeks they'll lose a quarter of a million. They'll get a few acres of mud and craters, a kilometre or two of Hun trenchlines. The Huns fall back and dig new trenches.

We were taken into the Somme and I don't remember much. I do remember thinking it couldn't get any worse, but that was before Ypres, Passchendaele and Messines. Or the Somme again in 1918 — or Amiens. Later battles, wading even deeper in blood, filth and mud.

Twenty dead from my company, twice that wounded. Bright, Connor, Appleyard, family men who led decent, better lives than I did. But me, Moran the street lout, came through without a scratch. And when enough of us were dead, the generals pulled us out.

But they couldn't pull the memories from our heads. The endless storm of shelling and the black mud that sucked us down. The German machine-guns that cut us down in lines. The bodies of men we knew, going swollen and black. Dead horses with their legs sticking up. Sergeant McKinnon, headless on the wire. Bloody water in the shell-craters, frozen to pink ice. Bodies, bits of bodies and the sweet horrible stink of decay.

Rowlands bawling, 'Dig, dig, dig!' as the shells screamed towards us. Shellfire that shook the mud into bottomless black porridge. We dug though — trenches, filled sandbags, fortified shell-craters — because if you dug, you had a chance. Mud slimed black all over us, in our food, in our stomachs.

'Diggers', the British called us, but it was a salute.

Yes, and Duncan missing, thought dead. He turns up when it's all over, says he was with another unit. He can't remember which but Brasso and me cover for him. He's a mate and I wouldn't land my worst enemy in front of Creel. We didn't see too much of him, either.

So we were pulled back to a rest area and reinforcements came from the big training camp at Etaples. They were clean-shaven and well-fed. Their uniforms and equipment were spotless. They looked at us like we were dead men returning from hell.

There was only one good thing about the Somme, and one reason why I don't remember too much of it. Because those other more bloody battles just overwhelmed it, like a body lost in the mud.

And the good thing?

Not knowing at the time that we would see far worse.

We get a new sergeant, Gorman, just promoted, grumpy bugger, thinks his new stripes make him king. Rowlands did try and get me the job. Creel had a hundred objections except the right one — he doesn't like me. Sod that, I'm OK as corp and Gorman's realising he needs me, after a couple of patrols and a Hun trench-raid.

We're back in the front line, the offensive over, both sides taking it easy. As easy as it ever gets. Autumn or colder. One of those quiet times, the stink still thick enough to cut with a knife. We get two visitors —

Creel — almost a stranger this far up — and another bloke; who's got 'civvy specialist' all over him. One of those people the army gives a commission to, because they know all about some special kind of crap. He tells us his, and Brasso rolls up his eyes. I swear even Rowlands gives a quiet groan.

Grenades.

The Huns had a good grenade when this war started, we didn't at Gallipoli — we used jam tins, packed with powder and scrap metal. Since then we've seen a dozen types, most of 'em bloody useless.

Lemon grenades, Ball, Oval, Pitcher, Egg — the

French have something called a 'Bracelet.' Parachute grenades (which came floating down on our heads) even one called a Hairbrush.

And percussion grenades. They go off on contact and the officer who demonstrated them at Etaples said be very careful. Tapped the table with one as he did and blew himself into little bits. Normally we try and get Hun grenades, 'potato-mashers', *they're* more reliable.

This guy is demonstrating three new types. Discus, Senior and one shaped like wheel. He's tall, big spectacles, uniform loose and helmet nearly around his ears, lumping a big canister. He's keen though, grins and remarks it whiffs a bit, should we complain to the Huns? Very bloody funny, nobody laughs.

The Germans know we have visitors and lob some pineapples over, by way of saying hello. Creel is starting to look nervous, snaps to get on with it. Brasso — who can chuck bombs with the best of them — is hauled in to do the honours.

Discus first. It's meant to be thrown like one and he chucks it well into no-man's land. Doesn't work, it's spinning when it explodes and the pellets and scrap come whizzing back overhead. 'Not much use if it shoots stuff at us,' murmurs Rowlands.

Next the 'Senior', and our civvy bloke explains. It has sharp corners, designed to angle in flight and go around corners, like a boomerang. 'If it's a boomerang, the Aussies should be testing it,' mutters Pig. Creel says shut up, and tells Brasso to wipe that smirk off his face.

Now the civvy bloke is pulling the covers off a strange contraption of wood, pulleys and cord. A catapult, he says, weapon of ancient warfare adapted to modern times, to launch grenades. Even Rowlands looks doubtful at this one; we've tested these bloody things before.

So he winds it back and Brasso fits the Senior. Twang and up it goes, curves in a neat line back towards us — boom. More scrap and pellets shower down. The civvy guy yelps, as one pings off his helmet, and mutters about more testing needed.

Finally the wheel-shaped grenade. Our civvy (a little less bright now) explains it will wheel towards the Hun lines. He loads it into the launcher and Brasso releases it. Another twang, it sails over the parapet and hits no-man's land, moving. Rowlands and I track it on periscopes. It wheels towards the Jerry lines, goes around a shell-crater and returns towards us.

'Coming back! Everyone down!' he yells.

I stand up and snap-shot, duck. The thing explodes, bits of rotting filth shower around us — nearly as filthy as the look I get from Creel. But that's the end of the testing. One of the catapult lines is somehow cut — Brasso can be quick with a knife — so Creel and the civvy go back down to the second trenches. Another few thousand quid of design gone up in smoke.

'I don't know why the Huns bother throwing grenades at us,' says Rowlands. 'Simpler to let us blow ourselves up.'

Even Gorman cracks a laugh at that one.

Mills bomb   Potato masher

WE WERE BACK in the second-line trenches in December — still close to the front on Christmas Eve when the guns fell silent for one day. It was strange to hear nothing. Cold as the grave and the snow covering all the frozen black in dazzling white.

Old hands told us that, last year, the Huns came out of their trenches. They met our men in no-man's land, exchanged gifts and chatted like men with no argument. Like we did with the Turks at Gallipoli on a truce day; finding out they were ordinary blokes like us who just wanted to get out of this with a whole skin.

Anyway, being mates with the Hun must've made the generals pee in their britches. We had orders this year to shoot any Hun who showed his face and —

from an odd rifle-shot or two — so did they. Then a new sound came across the white trenches and shell-craters. Singing.

'Hey,' says Pig, 'listen to them!'

'Just Christmas carols,' says Brasso, blowing on his mittened hands. 'Our boys sing them too, Pig.'

We're huddled around a little stove in the dug-out. An icy wind flaps the sacking across the entrance. We have on layers of clothing and heavy sheepskin jackets, heads wrapped in scarves and caps — and we're still cold.

'Yeah, but that's our song.' Pig has only room for one idea in his head at a time. '"Silent Night", that's ours, right?'

Rowlands has smelled the tea and rum, comes to the entrance of our shelter. He's a good officer, gets a mug and sips it. His lips are red and chapped. 'Actually it was a German song first,' he said.

'It's ours now,' growled Pig. 'Got English words, even. They shouldn't be singing it no more.'

Rowlands rolls his eyes. 'You have my permission to nip over and tell them.'

Pig just grunts. I take my tin mug and go outside. I breathe in the icy cold wind and feel like something has changed in me. I thought I had life pegged after Gallipoli, but things are still changing.

One of the new boys, wrapped from head to toe, is shivering beside a Vickers gun. I give him the last of my tea. Charcoal fumes come from the gun heater. The Vickers would freeze solid otherwise.

In the far distance, the Germans are on the last verse. Even I know that one, it was Mum's favourite. She'd wrap oranges in the blue lining paper from tea-chests and put them under a pine branch. We'd have a good supper of sausages and bacon and even Dad would drink himself under without belting us.

Sleep in heavenly peace ...

This peace will end tomorrow. The white waste-land will go black with shell-craters and the strange silence will be replaced by the normal sound of guns. My strange thoughts too, wondering about the new year; because I've always lived for the moment. 1917, I'll be nineteen years old. Nobody's winning this war. The new year will bring more of the same.

Sleep in heavenly peace ...

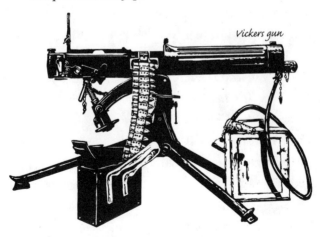

Vickers gun

New Zealand, 1940

My LUNGS SEEM *worse, like they're raw, filling with something. Not hurting, Jessica's touch took that away, but I'm still coughing. A white figure in the darkness, Nurse Tanner? No, a man in a white coat.*

Bloody doctors! Wouldn't know a self-inflicted wound if they fell over one!

'Pardon, old chap?'

Must've said something because the doctor bends over. The young bloke on our ward, not that stiff pommy prick who was gunning for Sullivan. Hospital, met Jessica there ... Betty. *He takes my pulse and goes.*

'Won't last the night,' he whispers to Nurse Tanner, but I hear him.

This is what I tackled those machine-gun nests for. And that bloody fool Churchill is running the show now, God help us. And Turkey's not in the war, Japan's on the other side. Things change.

'Jacko?'

It's Duncan. In that plain khaki jacket I saw him last wearing. A butcher in civvy life, he couldn't handle the butchery on the Somme. His lips are pressed that tight way as though he's not sure he's welcome.

'Course you are, Duncan. Sorry for what happened. That bastard Creel, he got his — after a fashion. *Duncan nods, smiles — an eye blink and he's gone.*

My mother won't come. I can't remember her, no

picture. Fat in her last years, old shapeless clothes, smelling of gin. At least she tried, even though her embrace was always boozy.

Betty, still alive I think, married some rich lawyer, her kids old enough to fight now.

Eileen, she won't come.

The gold walls of Buckingham Palace, the wet grey London streets. I'm coughing again, a cool hand on my forehead.

'I'm here, Jacko.'

Jessica Collingwood again. It's weird, like I'm floating a moment, the thoughts bursting in my head. Bright thoughts, like those anti-aircraft shells they fired at night, glowing in the sky like fireworks — flaming onions, that pilot called them. Wonder if he lasted the war?

More coughing that shakes my body like I'm choking. Full of colour and those sharp painful thoughts. Dark memory, flashing and flickering like shell-bursts at night, bursting in the darkness like those flaming onions.

Sleep in heavenly peace!

Flanders, 1917

There's a long, long trail awinding ...

— *soldiers' song*

ANOTHER NEW intake, conscripts, not the willing heroes of 1914. Etaples camp does a good job, but they still have to learn how to survive in the trenches. More names — Walker, Cooke, Norris, Sullivan, another joker. *Bingham, face-down in that shell-crater.* We're in the second line, even so, they flinch a bit at the sound of guns. Good, being nervous will help keep them alive.

Duncan's getting a check-up at base hospital. Swears his Gallipoli stomach wound is playing up and I believe him. But if you look healthy, you are healthy. The doctors have their orders, too.

There's a spare bed in our dug-out and in comes one of the new intake; small and skinny with little, thick-lensed glasses balanced on a button nose. We look at him in silence.

He salutes. 'Private Cuthbert Edmonds reporting for duty, sir.'

Brasso and I look at each other. 'You don't salute or sir me, I'm a corporal.'

He looks about sixteen — are they scraping the bottom of the barrel at home? I jerk a thumb at the spare bunk and he sits down, gives a little grin. Nice rubber overshoes that Brasso's already eyeing.

'It's good to be in the thick of things,' he says, and seems to mean it.

'You're not, yet,' says Brasso. We're playing two-handed poker and he's just scored Dead Willi's watch.

'Front line next week. You will be then.'

'I can't wait,' he says.

Brasso looks at me, taps his head. Mad.

Cuthbert Edmonds begins unpacking. He brings out bread, gooey French cheese and a bottle of wine, offers to share. Of course we let him.

'I've brought a board game with me,' he says. 'Something to wile away the idle hours.'

'The Huns usually do that for you,' I reply. 'What's the game?'

'Snakes and Ladders.'

Brasso is seized with a sudden fit of coughing and nearly drops his cards.

Cuthbert beams at us, polishing his glasses. 'I know everyone's got a nickname. Mine's Frog.' He gestures to the weather outside, removing his overshoes. 'An amphibian, rather appropriate for this weather.'

I can't spell amfib-something. We finish the game, Brasso shuffles the cards and smiles nicely at Frog. 'We mainly play cards,' he says. 'Fancy a game?'

'Oh, certainly,' says the innocent lamb. 'I play a little whist.'

'Whist it is,' grins Brasso, shuffling the deck again. 'Penny a point?'

It doesn't take long — about half an hour to be exact. I don't play whist so I just watch. Brasso is grinning and winning, then the Frog does something called '*abondance declarée*'. It's like running into kings and aces at poker, and Brasso's smile is wiped right off.

Frog rakes in the money, remarks cheerfully how he enjoyed the game, but there's nothing to spend the money on. Have we any suggestions on what he should do with it?

He's surprised and a bit offended when Brasso tells him.

'Jacko. D'you reckon I've got trench foot?'

We are back in the front line. Summer. Winter and summer are both bloody awful in the trenches for different reasons. The stench of all those unfrozen bodies, the flies and sticky heat. The lice multiply and I'm scratching.

I still think about Eileen, still feel let down. Maybe another letter? No, months since the first and she never answered that. Pig has removed his boots and is pulling off his socks. Sullivan rolls his eyes and chokes, both hands on his throat. 'Gas warning … gas … ahhhh …' and collapses, cross-eyed.

Pig chucks his last sock at Sullivan who dodges, laughing. He sticks his foot out. 'What d'you think, Jacko?'

I've seen enough horrible sights in this war. 'You just took your socks off, didn't you?'

'Yeah.'

'Did your toes fall off? Because you haven't got trench foot until then. Army regulations.'

British and German aeroplanes are scrapping overhead — 'dogfighting' they call it. They whirl around like stiff-winged birds and one falls, with smoke trailing behind.

'Us or a German?' asks Frog.

Brasso raises looted binoculars. 'Hun. A bob says the pilot jumps.'

'You're on,' says Norris. Government clerk before the war.

The plane is falling quickly now, nose and wing covered in flames. A little black object — a man — suddenly tumbles out. He drops faster than the plane, twisting in midair, faster as he nears the ground — Norris flicks over the shilling.

'Smart bugger, better than roasting,' says Pig.

'Another one.' Brasso glued to the binoculars. 'No, one of ours.'

We don't bet on our planes. So we watch it tumble, flaming and sparking like a firework. The pilot doesn't jump, but sometimes they just shoot themselves. The fight is breaking up now. One more plane is trailing smoke but it stays in the air. The show's over for today, and it's too bloody hot to think about Eileen.

Flanders poppies

THERE'S A TINGLE inside me, that cold prickly feeling as I move along the trench at midnight. Press the point of the Turk bullet in my pocket, make sure I tread on the loose duckboard. Little things, habits. Because it's near midnight and I'm getting ready for another stint in no-man's land.

I'm nearly at the observation post and bump into Rowlands, on his rounds. '*Ach, der Todeshund*,' he says.

'Sir?'

'Last Jerry prisoner told us your nickname. *Todeshund*. Means "hound of death".'

'*Hund* also means 'dog', pipes up Frog, on sentry-go, who likes to air his knowledge. 'Death-dog.'

Hound sounds better than dog. Frog gets a look and turns hastily away. Rowlands and I walk up to the end-post. I tell myself I'll hear the splash of duckboards underfoot when I return. Press my thumb over the bullet again. Rowlands talking in a whisper …

'What were those people … the Valkyries?'

What the hell is he on about? Last check, ammo, canteen, some hard-tack, no real appetite when I'm killing.

'Viking mythology,' he says. 'They were the choosers of the slain in battle.'

A patrol is coming in with Sergeant Gorman. Ex-schoolteacher, not a bad soldier now. He whispers that it's quiet as the grave. Good place for a death-hound then. Rowlands smiles, whispers again. 'No, they chose *after* the battle. You *choose* who to slay, right?'

What is he on about — choosing, slaying? Then I realise it's his way of wishing me luck without saying so. He knows I don't like that. So I nod, he nods back.

'See you, corp.'

'Sir.'

And I'm out into the muddy black stench and littered ground; shell-craters and barbed wire that is *my* ground. I breathe in like a hunting animal, like a hound sniffing for prey.

IT TAKES AN hour to reach one of my hides — a splintered mass of boards that was once a farm-cart. My little burrow is scraped underneath. I check it for booby-traps in case the Huns have found it. The little string across the entrance is unbroken. I wriggle inside and stretch out on the soft warm mud.

This is a good hide. Three hours till dawn, then the Hun patrols will come out, the work parties to do the jobs that can be done at night. Or returning from night-work, tired and maybe careless. Thinking they are safe for another day, thinking about a hot breakfast in their bomb-proof shelter. Thinking of sleep.

I am waiting for them. The careless ones.

Choosing the slain?

DAWN COMES and so do my targets.

Three of them in leather work-jackets, and inside a minute all will be dead. A wiring party, they are stringing communications from a forward listening post; close to their main trenchline and thinking they are safe.

They're not. Jacko Moran, their *Todeshund*, is tracking them over his rifle sights and they are living their last moments.

They've stopped a moment in the safety of a shell-crater, catching their breath for the final scramble over the parapet, even passing a canteen. Bad mistake. One, with a little black moustache, takes off his helmet and mops his forehead. A fatal mistake.

I settle carefully. This job is like poker sometimes, bluff and double-bluff. I shot here last week, moved on, shot and moved on, creating a pattern but doubling back. So here it comes, you careless Huns — your own personal Valkyrie.

The black-moustached one is still wiping his face. My rifle-sights go from him to a fat, red-cheeked one, then to the third, young and moon-faced, with earphones on under a cloth cap. So ... choosing.

The fat man first. Sweat is trickling down his face and his throat bulges over his tunic collar. His Adam's apple bobs as he drinks from the canteen, and I can almost hear him swallowing.

I squeeze the trigger.

The bullet punctures the canteen, jerking it from his hand. I work the bolt. The second shot sends the corporal's helmet bouncing along the ground; the third clips Moon-face's earphone — oops, think I got the ear too.

They are yelling. Diving for cover. I slither backwards out of the hide, having to move quick and silent now. But nobody knows where the shots came from, and at least they're alive to yell.

Maybe I should have shot them but I wanted just once to choose. And I actually find myself grinning as I work back through no-man's land, nearly get caught in a mortar barrage and wait for night.

Rowlands is by the forward post again, Frog back on sentry. I tell him about the new wiring and a few other little things I've seen. I end the report, 'Corporal Valkyrie didn't slay anyone today, sir.'

Frog sniggers for some reason and Rowlands waits till we are back in the main trench before speaking. Then his lips twitch, like he's hiding a smile. 'Corp,' he says, 'Valkyries were women.'

He goes on to his dugout and I stand looking after him. Women! Why couldn't the soddin' bugger have told me? I'll have to get hold of Frog now before he tells anyone.

Brasso would never stop laughing.

Dog skull

81

'IT SAYS HERE that a Great White Shark is per — per — Pig pauses and Frog leans over.

'Persecuting,' he says.

Pig nods and reads on, frowning. The *New York Times*, left by a visiting Yank officer. Pig always frowns when he reads. It's another blazing hot day, full of stink and flies, but we're back to second trench-lines so Parapet Joe and Hun raiding patrols can be forgotten. Best of all, Creel, is away on leave.

'It says the shark ate four people off the New Jersey coast. Then went twenty miles inland to a town.'

'How'd it get inland?' asks Frog smiling. 'Take a train?'

'Swam upriver.' Pig has no sense of humour. 'Ate two people there.'

'Trust the bloody Yanks to go swimming when there's a shark around,' laughs Brasso. 'They must be stupid.'

'Then it tried to eat some bloke in a boat. He clubbed it to death.'

'Does it say when the Yank army's coming over?' I asked.

There's a lot of talk about that. Almost half a million, we've heard, tipping the war in our favour. Maybe. Two Yank officers came through the front line before we pulled out. 'Observers', smart as hell in brown tunics and whipcord breeches. Young and bright, said things were 'OK' or 'a genuine article' or a 'gosh-durn situation'.

We showed them a fixed-rifle point. One says, 'A sniper — the genuine article?' and *stands to look*! A Hun bullet takes the top of his head right off, cap and all. His mate goes green at all that blood and brains and bursts into tears.

We got a shot of rum into him and wrapped his mate in a blanket. We even blazed off at the Huns, who did not reply — probably too busy laughing. Getting shot, eaten by sharks.

Stupid.

Rowlands has come up and takes the paper for the crossword. 'Half a million Doughboys,' he says. 'That'll make a nice difference.'

'Doughboy' is a nickname for Yanks, like 'Tommy' for British and whatever's rude enough for Aussies. 'Wonder how many when the Huns have finished with them?' I say.

Rowlands squats down. 'Well, the British said to send them over in shirt-sleeves, we'll kit them out, some weeks' basic, then pack them off to the front line.'

We look at each other. How generous of the Brits. Half a million more men to use up; the generals must've thought all their Christmases had come at once.

'Of course the French wanted a slice of that,'

says Rowlands. 'And the Italians put in for twenty divisions.'

'What did the Yanks say, sir?' Frog 'sirs' more often than anyone.

'They said, forget it, our boys aren't for hire. Their new general — Pershing — said they'd come over as an army when they were good and trained.' He goes whistling back to his dugout.

So the Yanks will come when they're ready? On their terms? Not so stupid after all.

Rowlands arranged some leave for Jim Duncan and he's back, just when we're moving up to the front again. Brasso and me have a talk but he swears he's all right now. He's not, he's twitchy as hell; scared, and too scared to admit it. I break one sworn habit and ask Creel for his assistance.

Useless. 'There is a crisis, corporal. Every man is needed and the doctors quite simply say there is no such thing as shell-shock. There is such a thing as soldiers trying to dodge their duty and,' he says smoothly, 'that is a very different matter indeed.'

Well you'd know all about dodging duty! I salute and leave, longing to wipe the smirk off his chubby pink face.

Rowlands would like to help but his hands are tied. Says can we just keep an eye on Duncan, help him. Of course we'll do that. But I know, just know, the poor bugger's about to crack.

Brasso has never forgotten how Frog creamed him at whist. He even got a book on cards to read the whist section, and to find out just how Frog pulled that '*abondance*' thing.

'Got him pegged now,' he says to me.

Frog is quite happy to have a rematch. He loves being one of the boys. Brasso ups the table stakes and we settle down to play. I pair with Frog, Duncan with Brasso. It's good to see him playing, laughing — he seems like his old self. Maybe things will be all right.

Brasso sits with that blank look of his and takes trick after trick. He ups the ante to a shilling a point. Frog is looking very concerned behind his spectacles. Then, with Brasso about to crow in triumph, he puts down an ace of diamonds. Then a queen and jack of diamonds.

Brasso looks like he's been smacked in the face with a sandbag. Frog explains how Brasso's king could not have been guarded, with only three other cards. He beams and offers to give Brasso lessons, then rakes in a pot of twenty pounds! Frog's not sure what to do with all his winnings. So he donates it to a relief fund!

Brasso doesn't speak to him for a week.

Whizz-plop! Whizz-plop! That bursting sound like no other shell exploding. 'Gas!' goes the shout, then there's the tonk-tonk-tonk of the gas bell.

And always the sick horror when you hear it, grabbing your gas-mask as the yellow clouds form. Mustard gas, doesn't kill, just makes you cough your lungs red. The Huns want sick men who have to be looked after, not dead ones who can be buried.

So it fills the trench like the greasy breath of hell itself. Thick, oily and yellow, forming in droplets on your mask. You breathe loudly in your own ears, man the firing step and wait for the Huns.

And they come, sometimes gas-masked, sometimes not; so you hope the wind will change and blow it back. The stuff settles on your uniform and leaves oily filth everywhere. Cooke doubles over, coughing, mask on too late. I pull him onto a dugout, yell at the men to keep firing.

Another huddled in a dugout entrance, rifle on the ground; gas-mask in place so I pull him out. Duncan, his eyes rolling wildly behind the mask. I push him to the firing step, bawl at him to shoot.

We were just in time. A short fight but bloody. A last Hun bullet throws Sergeant Gorman back, dead. Rowlands yells for me to take over. When I go back, Duncan is gone. We find him huddled in the communication trench, shaking like hell.

I haul him back and Rowlands turns a blind eye

— this time — but warns me it can't go on. The other men know what's happening; they have to stand and fight. If Duncan runs again, it'll be once too often.

I'm made up to acting-sergeant. Gorman goes to one of those open graves at the cemetery and a fernleaf headstone. I almost wish a German bullet had got Duncan.

Next day the Huns shell us again. They have a special hate for this sector because it's where *Todeshund* has his kennel. And it happens. In the screaming noise, explosions and showers of earth, Duncan takes off and doesn't stop at the communication trench.

The military police pick him up two weeks later.

Rowlands gets the news and calls me in. 'Creel's preferring charges,' he says quietly. 'Desertion in the face of the enemy.'

We know what that means. So it won't be a German bullet that gets Duncan.

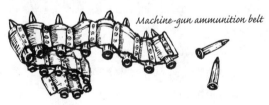

Machine-gun ammunition belt

IT'S A GREAT day. Early rain has cooled the morning sun a little, and back here, away from the lines, the birds sing sweetly. There's a stone wall behind headquarters

87

and a few clucking hens to be shooed away. Puddles of rainwater steam in the sun.

I've never seen so many officers together, all spruced up, their boots gleaming and brass buttons shining like gold. Most have the red shoulder-tabs of the staff; more than you would ever see up the line. Creel is strutting importantly around them.

Rowlands looks at his watch. He's tense. 'Make it quick, sergeant.'

He doesn't have to tell me that. No volunteers, just ten good riflemen with orders to shoot straight — or get a bullet from me. A chair is placed in front of the stone wall, even the square of paper and pin.

Somewhere a clock is striking ten as I go around to the stables. The MP sergeant is a brick-red Pom with waxed black moustache. 'Snivelling little bugger's got a skinful of rum,' he remarks. 'Should be all right unless he wets himself.'

These last words end in a little choke because I've rammed him up against the wall, my hand under his plump chin, my face close to his. 'That man's seen more bloody action than you ever will! So treat him with respect!'

He's looking murder but just chokes and glowers when I let him go. Mutters that I'll hear about this, but leads the way without speaking.

Jim Duncan does have a skinful. He's standing though, in uniform, his tunic buttoned. Gives me a crooked smile, even a 'Hi, Jacko,' but there's a terrified glint in his eyes when they strap his arms.

'Come on, Jim,' I say quietly.

I'm a front-line soldier and we do the fighting. I should be the one most disgusted with Duncan, not some traffic-directing military cop. But I've nearly been where he went. When your nerve cracks and that silent screaming starts loud inside you.

The sun is warmer now. My boots splash in a puddle, Duncan's boots splash behind me. The firing party line, the officers, their brasswork glinting. Duncan is white, sick-looking, as they sit him down, tie him to the chair. The white paper is pinned to his chest.

'Good luck, mate.' *Good luck?*

'Blindfold?' asks one MP.

A last eyeline between Duncan and me as the black cloth goes over his face. His lips move, sucking in air through the black cloth; he's trying not to shake. The chaplain whispers his rubbish then we go back, our footsteps sloshing in more puddles. My guts are wrenching in a tight knot.

Creel ordered me here, the —

The sentence is read out. Duncan sitting in the straps, sags as though already dead. His head bowed, the white paper flutters on his chest.

'Attention. Present arms. Fire!'

The volley crashes out, the smoke blows in my face. The clucking hens are shocked to silence. Duncan and the chair are flung back against the wall; go down in a huddle of limbs and broken wood. The white paper on his chest is shredded and sodden red.

Good shooting, thank God.

Even so, the army wants full measure. A last bullet in the head to make sure. So Rowlands has to go up with his revolver, I go with him. The body huddled, unmoving; the blindfold slipped to show one staring eye. Does it roll slightly at us? The Webley makes a smaller sound, the hens are still silent.

James Duncan is well and truly dead.

The spectators drift away. It's interesting to see a man shot; there's none in watching his bullet-riddled body. Colonel Fields is the only one who looks unhappy — he knew Duncan in Gallipoli. Creel — pink-cheeked and smooth-faced — murmurs a 'well-done' to Rowlands. Glances at me, sees the look in my eyes and turns away.

I watch him walk off. He's careful to step around the puddles so as not to get mud on his nice polished boots.

One day, Creel … one day.

The firing party and MPs get eggs and bacon and a few bottles of rum. The MP sergeant sits beside me, chewing on a mouthful of bacon. 'Not too bad. Done a baker's dozen of these, this year. *Pour encourage* others, eh?'

His bad French for 'to encourage the others'. OK, so he's shot thirteen and Duncan makes fourteen.

I don't want to sit with him or to drink. I get some coffee and go outside.

A truck goes past with a wooden box on the back with Duncan in it. I don't know where they buried him or what they told his folks. The morning sun is hot and the hens are clucking again. A burst of laughing comes from the farmhouse where the officers are having a late breakfast. I long to end it with a grenade.

Duncan fought through Gallipoli till he copped that Turk bullet and he was a good mate. And I've shook with fear like him and wanted to run. It's like a bad dream but the hens are clucking and soon I'll be shooting Germans again. Another burst of laughter and I remember Creel skipping the puddles in his polished boots.

One day!

Kitchener poster

'MORAN! YOU'RE confirmed as sergeant. That means you're no longer acting.'

'Thank you, Lieutenant Rowlands. Honoured, sir.'

'I'm sure you are, but you're stuck with it. Oh, and it's Captain Rowlands now.'

'Congratulations, sir. And Captain Creel, sir?'

'Is now Major Creel.'

'He'll have more time to attend his important conferences, sir.'

'Don't push your luck, Moran. Even sergeants only get away with so much.'

'Sir.'

'And Brasso is made up to corporal.'

'He'll be delighted, sir.'

'No, he won't. But he's stuck with it too.'

And we're all stuck with the bloody war.

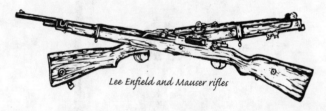

Lee Enfield and Mauser rifles

THE MACHINE-GUN opens with a jarring clack and we go to earth. Too late for the three men, two thrown back like puppets, Walker screams, gutshot; he's bleeding to death.

And I'm cursing like hell because I saw this coming. So did Rowlands, I'm sure. It was a local attack but the Germans gave way and we got into their trenches. Creel shrilled with delight at the easy victory (and promotion out of the front line) and told us to press on, with visions of routing the Hun back to Berlin.

No chance. The Huns are smarter than Creel and their front line is just shell-holes and a few connecting trenches. Second line is their real defence, they've sucked us in and even Creel knows what they'll do now. Counter-attack on our flanks (enfilade is the fancy term) and cut us off. Then finish us off.

So I hit the mud cursing, the bullets whiplash up and down. And I spot something, so does Rowlands. The Huns have sprung their ambush too soon. Rowlands is yelling for the men to pull back and there's no sign of Creel. And I'm flat in the mud, the Spandau bullets whipping overhead, suddenly angry — *why do I think of the old man at times like this!*

Gut-wrenching, stubborn and burning anger, bloody Hun bullets everywhere, fatal to lose your bloody temper because then you're bloody dead — *I'm taking off my belt to you, boy!* Part of me raging, the other part cold, the racket deafening. I hold up a grenade, signal to Rowlands. He nods and nudges Frog, who has the light Lewis machine-gun — get ready.

I belly forward, can see the Hun machine-gun and spiked helmets showing just over the sandbags. Wishing I'd brought the Mannlicher, wiping mud from the breech of my Enfield. Fire once, work the bolt, fire twice. Again and again, all five shots and for a moment they duck — all the moment I need.

Grenades ready, pulling out the pins. Getting up, mud splashing, nearly turning my ankle. *Three-second fuse, throw them!* One, two, three. Two explode inside, one in midair. Running now, fourth grenade up and throwing.

They're not all dead. A gunner is swinging the Spandau towards me — bloody long barrels those guns have. The fourth grenade explodes and I do a header over the sandbags. Six in the crew, one dead, two wounded. Whack one with the rifle. An officer, bloodied and muddy, brings up his Luger. I knock it from his hands, boot him in the face.

The machine-gunner, a stout man, with a thick fair moustache, turns, grimacing, and utters a high scream as I drive the bayonet in. *Hell, you were killing my mates* — it sticks, I have to fire into him and jerk it loose, his tunic smouldering from the muzzle-blast. Rowlands scrambles in, Pig and Frog behind him.

'Good work, come on.'

No time to waste. Rowlands blows his whistle, pulling the men back as the Hun shellfire comes. The sound of bugles means the Germans are advancing. Another machine-gun opens up ahead, yammer-yammer. Cooke — wife and three kids — hits the mud dead.

My hot anger is gone, the cold rage still there.

Cooke was a good bloke. That stubborn driving force in me, like death doesn't matter. Frog fires the light Lewis, butt against his shoulder, his little face grimy and determined.

So I belly forward, the shells exploding around me. My foot gets caught in a tangle of barbed wire and I pull it free, leaving the boot behind. The Huns have seen me and the bullets lash up viciously. I bring up the Enfield and a bullet shatters the butt. Hell, that hurt! Splinters in my cheek, blood streaming in the mud — it only makes the cold anger worse.

There are mortars falling on us now. Pull out four more grenades. The German bugles are closer. Pulling out all the pins, *how long is three seconds?* I throw them — a horrible moment as I lose one in the mud, chuck it ahead just before it explodes. A sharp kicking pain under my chin.

Getting up, my bayonet bent. The last grenade throws up mud and blinds the Hun gunner as I throw one more. *Overarm, cricket at the wasteground, plank for a bat, stone for balls, those bloody great goldfish in the pools.* A mud-faced Hun in front, I fire. Another, young, shouting with terror, a third scrabbling for his own rifle. Even with the roar of battle, I can hear the flat shots of my Enfield. Eight dead, most by grenades.

The shellfire slackens because the Hun counter-attack is close. They're back over their front-line trenches and following us — those long grey overcoats and cloth-covered helmets. Supposed to be a second-rate battalion but there's lots of them, pressing us hard.

My throat is cracked with shouting, cheek and chin jabbing with pain, ribs like they've been kicked. One foot running blood, the sock ripped to shreds. Lucky the mud is soft. My ears are singing in the din and an odd glassy feel takes over. *Get your mucking head shot off!* I'm good at this, you old bugger. And I am, so think — *think!*

Frog is working the Lewis well but there's no easy way to pull back. Rowlands, down the line, is signalling frantically to disengage. Now the Germans are throwing those long-handled 'potato-mashers' of theirs. Attacking in sections, firing as they come, under good control.

A new boy, Ritchie, goes down, then Fulcher with his knee shattered. That will slow us further. The Huns are moving out on either side to outflank — murder us in the cross-fire.

Get my mucking head shot off? *Well it's my mucking head!* I scramble back into the wrecked German gun pit, pull the dead gunner off the Spandau and yell for the others to get moving. I pull the Spandau around — the Huns make good weapons — and rest the tripod on the back sandbags.

'Get moving!' I shout.

'Jacko!'

'Sergeant Moran to you.' May as well pull rank for the last time. 'Get them moving, corporal!'

I drag over the belts of ammunition. The belt-feed is different but I get it hooked up. Glancing around I see the others moving back. The closer ones aren't bothering about cover now. Shouting, officers yelling orders; their turn to take our trenches. *So where the hell is our artillery?*

Spandaus have a small trigger. I click back something that looks like the cocking bolt and wait. The German troops come closer, bayonets fixed, officers leading them on with swords. They're too close, I can't wait any longer.

The Spandau jolts like it's alive, with a flat, harsh crack. The officer spins around, sword flashing as it whirls from his hand. Most of the men on either side and behind drop to the ground like the well trained troops they are. Return fire, rifles and light machine-guns, the bullets phut past or stitch heavily into the sandbags.

I blaze away with the Spandau, keeping their heads down. Pause to grab one of their own potato-mashers, pull out the base and cord, throw. Then another, then back to the gun.

Why the hell do this? Courage, duty as senior non-com, self-sacrifice — none of that registers. It's rage, anger, seeing Duncan's bullet-riddled body. Wanting to hit out and hit out — and a stubborn cold detachment that keeps me thinking.

Artillery!

Minutes are passing, long minutes; the others will be back now, Rowlands can rally them to hold the trench. Me, I'll be a corpse, go swollen and black or get torn apart in the shellfire. What the hell. A fumble and clatter as a German soldier comes over the sandbags.

He should've chucked a grenade first! I drag the heavy gun bodily around, damn recoil would knock me over if I wasn't braced. Fire and he's flung back, the trigger clicks empty. No more ammunition, I throw the gun aside. Throw over the last two grenades, grab my Enfield, one clip left, *so I'll go down fighting!*

Another crash, an explosion ahead. Then another and another, mortar bombs; the express-train noise of a shell overhead. It explodes and a German helmet spins up into the air. Shells are landing all around — so get out! Over the sandbags, no Germans following now. I run back through no-man's land while all hell breaks loose around me.

Our trenchline ahead, leaping over the parapet and down on the duckboards. The boys there gape like I'm back from the dead. 'We thought you'd had it!' squeals Pig.

'I mucking should have. Which silly mucker called those shells on me?'

'This silly mucker,' comes Rowlands' voice. 'I thought you were dead too. Stupid mistake, eh, sarge?'

The shellfire is screaming overhead. Not many Germans will get back to their own trenches. Rowlands takes my arm and leads me back down the trench to a dugout. For some reason my legs are wobbly. 'Bloody well done, Moran,' Rowlands is saying quietly as we stop.

There are other officers there. Creel (who beat us all back) gives a 'well done', his lips tight like there's a bad taste in his mouth. The other officer steps forward, binoculars in one hand.

'Absolutely wizard, sterling effort!' He's a real Gawd-help-us pukka Pom. 'Spiffing work, seeking death in the cannon's mouth — what? One word for you, sergeant — pluck!'

For the moment I think he used a word that rhymes with pluck. He's young, with one of those big moustaches and a bigger grin on his well-fed face. His open overcoat shows the red staff tabs on his shoulders, so he's a captain. They don't often come up this far.

'Yes, good show,' says Creel, something still tasting bad. 'Now get yourself seen to.'

It's then I realise a bullet scraped my arm and my sleeve is red with blood. My chin is gashed by grenade fragments, my fingers seem broken from handling that gun and my chest is bruised where it hammered against me. One boot missing, my foot torn to the bone by barbed wire.

'Yes, by all means,' says the staff Pom. 'Here — my hand.'

He holds it out, nice brown leather gloves, I

notice. I pause though, and Creel interrupts sharply. 'Captain Lord Fairleigh-Granger is holding out his hand, sergeant.'

A title, double-barrelled name and 'spiffing', 'wizard' — the unknown language of the upper class. I'm about to give him my best 'get stuffed' look because no self-respecting front-line soldier likes a staff officer — and not even Creel can make something of it. Then a wonderful wicked thought comes to mind.

I smile and take his hand. 'I'm a bit bloody sir, didn't want you mucked.'

'Oh, be damned to that, honour's mine, sergeant. Action of the tiger what? You're full of the right stuff. Hector and Lysander, don't you know?'

He means it. Like patting a dog or tipping some-one. So I give him a brave smile, even remember to wince a little. 'We've all got to do our best, sir, to keep Jerry on the back foot.'

'Spoken like a bally Trojan! Absolute bulls-eye! Bang on! Top hole!'

The slightly-wounded warrior gives him another brave smile. 'It's King and Country where I come from, sir.'

'Noble utterance, sergeant, noble!' He nods so vigorously that his monocle falls out. I'll swear his eyes are misted. 'Now get yourself patched up, old fellow. This won't go unnoticed, be damned it won't.'

I salute smartly and he salutes back. Creel —

who knows exactly what I'm doing — looks at me like I'm something unpleasant he just trod in. Rowlands has a hand over his mouth. He nods to me. I go, remembering to limp heavily. Not hard, my foot is hurting like hell.

Back up the trench, Brasso has a bottle — Brasso always has a bottle — so we drink and joke, but they're all a little strained now, even him. Pig just gapes at me.

'You saved all our hides, sarge,' says Brasso. 'Thanks.'

I have to knock that one on the head. 'Listen, I just wanted you muckers out of the way while I had a crack at them. All right?'

It's only the truth but Pig still gapes and Brasso doesn't object when I finish the bottle. The afternoon becomes blue evening and it's quiet — as it ever gets on the Western Front.

'First-aid station, Moran.' Rowlands has come up. 'Corporal, find Lieutenant Couch, get a watch together. I'll do a sentry inspection in half an hour.'

So the party breaks up. I don't mind first aid and a decent night's sleep. Rowlands looks at me, unsmiling.

'I never knew you were such a patriot, sergeant.'

'Sir?'

'But you do deserve a medal. It was a bloody fine bit of work, whatever your reasons.'

'I'm full of the right stuff, sir.'

'You're full of something. Now get moving.'

He grins, though, and I grin back. I head for the first-aid station, cold, aching, muddy and blood-stained. Remembering the look on Creel's face makes it all worthwhile.

spandau machine-gun

THE FIRST-AID station sends me on to a field hospital. My foot is hurting like hell. A lot of us are jammed in the ambulance, Sullivan, our company joker, nursing a bloody hand.

There's a long wait at the hospital. It's raining, men are lying outside on stretchers, line to line. Some are too badly wounded and the doctors just fill them with morphine. They die out there with the rain on their faces.

I don't mind the rain. My foot won't kill me and even if they cut it off, so what? No, mixed feelings there, I don't want a 'Blighty wound', one that will get me safe out of the war and back home. Sullivan has one, two fingers shot away, you need those to press a trigger. He's white-faced and silent, no jokes now.

The doctor finally gets to me. Pulls the splinters out of my cheek, murmurs 'superficial lacerations' to the tall dark-haired nurse beside him. She's in that long grey skirt and grey cape, edged with red. An odd look at me when I give my name and rank. Sergeant Moran.

She makes to speak then shuts her mouth. The doctor is asking me how I hurt my foot. Barbed wire, I say. Then he asks was an officer present when it happened and I click — *thinks it's self-inflicted!*

'Yes, doctor,' in my best *sod you* tone of voice, 'my captain saw it. 'Course this Hun Spandau was giving us stick, but I think so. Oh, and another captain, Staff Officer Lord Fairleigh-something, shook my hand and said I had pluck. Pluck, doctor.'

It's the way I say 'pluck' like the other word it rhymes with. He flushes, snaps that he's a major and addressed as 'sir.' And that bloody colonial troops have no manners. Then collects himself, an aside, 'Sorry, nurse.'

'Quite all right, sir,' she says with a New Zealand accent, a cool look at me. The doctor moves on and she pauses. 'Were you in Gallipoli, sergeant? Perhaps nicknamed Jacko?'

'Do I know you, miss?'

'No, but —'

The doctor calls her so she moves on, but she looks back several times. Sullivan is getting the same questions I did. A couple of orderlies appear and I'm taken in, a quick scrub, wounds dressed and a real bed. And slipping into deep, wonderful sleep.

NEXT MORNING the same doctor comes around the ward. Looks at my foot, three weeks, he says, then ready for duty. 'Can't wait, sir,' I say and give that too-cheerful grin that officers hate. Then I remember. 'How's Private Sullivan, sir? He was beside me.'

'Oh, with the fingers shot away?' A little too smooth. 'He's in a different ward.'

He walks on to the next man, the same dark-haired nurse with him. I don't get a look this time. No matter, I know her snooty type.

The nurse who comes to dress my foot later is much nicer. She's blonde, pretty, another New Zealander and new to all this. She hurts me a little, taking off the bandage, and apologises. I smile.

And while she's doing this and my arm, two staff officers turn up. Lieutenants, and they want an account of yesterday's action. I try to mention Creel disappearing but they're more interested in me. Why I attacked those gun pits, how many Germans, etc. In your own words, sergeant.

The nurse hears this, her eyes going round. When they're gone, she comes back and pretends to adjust my pillow. She smells starchy and antiseptic but good. And she thinks I'm quite a hero.

'Just doing my job, miss.'

Which was right but seems to impress her even more. A few painful stitches in my foot, but the doctor's right, I'll be up and about soon enough. So (I think) I may as well enjoy myself.

Betty Donaghy is her name, I ask her about

Sullivan and this 'other ward' business. She comes back the next day, looking very solemn. Sullivan is facing charges for a self-inflicted injury.

In the middle of battle? Crap, too many would have seen it and we'd let him be thrown to the wolves. When the doctor comes round again, I ask him — even try and sound respectful.

'Not my affair, sergeant,' he replies stiffly. 'Open and shut case. Left hand, two fingers shot off, classic.'

I keep my temper and try to explain. A soldier holds the rifle barrel with his left hand so it's exposed, unlike the right hand which is around the butt. So of course blokes are going to lose fingers. None of this makes any difference.

'I don't need a lecture on wounds, sergeant.' He shrugs and moves on.

I write a letter to Rowlands, then realise it will have to be forwarded through Creel, who won't care. Nor will the army. So Sullivan is headed for military prison. If he doesn't end up like Jim Duncan.

To encourage the others.

ONE WEEK goes, then another. I hate to admit it, but I'm getting around the ward, hobbling around with a stick and remembering to limp more painfully when I meet Betty Donaghy. She's a nice girl from a top family but one of those 'women's rights' people; socialism and the common man.

Well, that's me, common as hell and I'll have a few days' leave before returning. So when I suggest going out, she doesn't mind. She even likes the idea of going out with the brave sergeant.

I'm feeling good, too. There was this place outside Etaples, and since then some French tarts on leave; different though when you have to pay for it. And she is nice, I really like her; even though she does call me her '*beau ideal*'.

As the song goes, she'll melt in my arms.

I still see the tall dark-haired nurse sometimes and keep forgetting to ask Betty who she is. That turns out to be a serious mistake.

I can't sleep on my last night. Regular untroubled rest is all too strange. I'm used to catnapping in a dirty trench full of rats. A balcony fronts our ward and I get up, walk out onto it. We're not supposed to go out at night, but who cares? They can only send me back to the front.

Rowlands replied to my note on that lined yellow paper, a splash of candle-grease in the corner. I could almost hear the guns, see the dark, damp shelter. He said that he'd passed it on to Creel and we both knew what that meant. Sullivan would cop the full weight of army justice.

The front line is about twelve miles away but a strong wind is blowing. It brings the mutter of guns, as if war has a heartbeat, the constant flicker of lights and an aircraft droning overhead. The war never sleeps. A voice comes from the darkness behind me.

'Robert Moran. Jacko Turk-Hunter.'

All I can see is the red glow of a cigarette beside the door. Then she walks forward into the moonlight. The dark-haired nurse who's been giving me all those cool looks.

'How do you know me?'

She walks up, sits on the balcony rail and blows out more smoke. She indicates her cigarette. 'I picked up this habit in Egypt.'

'Nothing wrong with smoking.'

'An English doctor thinks it might cause lung illness and lower life expectancy.'

'Life expectancy?' I laugh. 'What the hell is that in the lines? Anyway, have we met?'

'No. A soldier from your platoon in Gallipoli mentioned you sometimes. Fred Muller — also called Hooter. And Harry Wainwright mentioned you in his letters to me.'

Oh yes. Now I had her pegged. Harry's girl, the nurse. Wainwright was one of those nice schoolboys who did join for God, King and Country. Gallipoli knocked out all that crap, made him a good mate. We buried him there before he could see his nurse again. And Hooter was back in New Zealand with a leg missing.

'And now we're both in Flanders, Sergeant Moran.'

I wasn't sure about her. One of those women who

act like they know every damn thing. My dad couldn't knock her around without getting a whack back. And I bet she never skipped a meal or went barefoot.

'You have a week's leave tomorrow?'

'Yes, I do —'What was her bloody name? 'Listen, who are you?'

'Jessica Collingwood.' Then she asked abruptly. 'Were you able to do anything about Sullivan?'

'No. Has to go through my company captain. Creel.'

'Rupert Creel?' She draws on her cigarette again. 'Then you and Sullivan have my profound sympathy.' She seems to mean it.

The gun-mutter goes on, it's cold and I don't want this conversation. So I shrug and turn to go inside. Her voice stops me.

'Stay away from Nurse Donaghy.'

'If you're making that an order, tell her.'

No smile. 'I know what you want. And she might even let you, thinking she has to. But she's not one of those sluts, plying their trade, sergeant. She's a nice girl with ideals and she'd hate herself afterwards.'

'So give her this sermon.'

'She wouldn't listen. Ideals.'

'Goodnight, Miss Collingwood, nice to have met you.'

Her voice tightens. 'She couldn't handle it, Moran. And I knew you'd be a bugger about this.'

'Well I'm just a common-as-cow-cakes non-com.' And I'm going in to bed, screw whatever she says now.

'Private Sullivan, I know one of the medical big-wigs. I could ask him to review the file. He doesn't like Doctor Prentice, your army major friend. He'd love to squash him.'

'All right.' I don't like Jessica Collingwood and I do like Betty Donaghy. But Sullivan is a mate and Creel is a yellow ratbag. And there are other girls. 'I'll drop Betty, but you'd better do something. Or I could write Betty and tell her about the nice fairy godmother.'

'You really are a hard basket, Moran.'

I go inside, take off the dressing-gown and slippers — first time I'd ever had those too. Jessica Collingwood walks through the ward without looking at me. Maybe she's right about me and Betty, but tomorrow morning is going to be tough.

I'M NEARLY DRESSED, my kit packed, when Betty comes into the ward. She smiles and looks so pretty in her starched white that I nearly forget Sullivan.

'We'll have a lovely time tomorrow, sergeant,' she says. 'I shall call you Robert.'

I don't know how to say this. 'Listen, I'm a sergeant. You're a lady.'

She smiles. 'Oh all that class system is nonsense. My brother and I have such heated rows with Daddy about it.'

It's not getting easier. 'I'm a sergeant, I want a skinful before I go up the line. And a girl who — gets paid and forgets me. So push off.'

I will never forget how white her face went. That sudden puzzled white, like somebody stopping a bullet. She fiddles with my medical chart a moment, mumbles something and leaves. And next moment a glass shatters on my iron bedstand.

It's thrown by my neighbour, a long-faced Irishman with heavy black eyebrows. He glares at me, all he can do, because his leg is broken. 'You damned rat, treating a decent girl like that.'

'What d'you expect from a mongrel En-Zedder,' calls an Aussie from the bed opposite. Like *they're* all flaming saints!

A few others glare or just look away. I feel my face set in a sullen scowl. Easy enough because I don't like what I did.

Jessica Collingwood comes stalking into the ward shortly after and sees the broken glass. The Irishman gets a broadside. She tells me the truck's waiting, I can go and she exits without another word.

I get my gear together. Nobody says goodbye.

So I GO BACK up the line in new kit from top to toe. Even a shiny new helmet and rifle, with the factory grease still on it. Swearing that if Brasso's lost my Mannlicher, I'll break it over his head. A bag full of bread, sausage and wine for the boys; a pound of coffee for Rowlands.

And guess who I meet first — in the second-line trenches of course. I ask him about Sullivan, and Creel replies, 'Under control,' like I don't exist.

Then the main trench; duckboards squelching underfoot, the stink, damp sandbags, tired, unshaven faces. 'Look who's back, the King's bad bargain. Jerry's been asking where you are, says the war's too quiet. Should've got them to chop your foot off, mate.'

So I grin, punch, slap shoulders; remember to duck under the fixed rifle. It's not home but it's where I live. I know this place and I know these men.

Some are missing, some new faces. McLean, 'Puha' to his mates. Soames, bricklayer's apprentice, Maynard, a tram-driver. Shaw and Mickle, out of college. Pig and little Frog, grinning happily.

Brasso and my mates celebrate with a little party. The wine, sausage and bread goes quickly, the cards come out. Frog suggests whist, Brasso suggests he go boil his head. We're in the middle of blackjack when Gregson, Rowlands' batman, goes past.

I shout to him, has he heard about Sullivan? He nods, yesterday, charges dropped.

We cheer, get him in for a mug of wine. I tell the others how it happened. Not about Betty, just that I put the hard word on a starchy up-herself nurse. Gregson nods, he's heard that through Rowlands.

'Sure. She went to one of the top guys a fortnight back. Said she'd cleaned the wound herself and there were no powder-burns.'

The others slap my shoulders, tell me I'm a good mate. We go on with the game but suddenly I'm off my cards. A fortnight! I was putting the screws on Jessica Collingwood for something she'd already done. I'd dropped Betty Donaghy for nothing.

And she had the cheek to call *me* a hard basket!

The front line has fallen quiet, the way it does sometimes. We still had a few 77 and 5.9 shells sailing over. Mortars, without which no day would be complete, and Parapet Joe to sing a goodnight lullaby of bullets.

One of those unspoken, unofficial truces goes into force. No stick from you and no stick from us. A Hun soldier calls across from no-man's land. 'Let's take a week off, Vernsleeves.' But we have to keep up appearances for visiting staff, so they fire a white flare and we fire a red one. That means get down and look serious. A few pineapples and the Spandaus undo the stitching on our sandbags.

We sit tight and it passes. Visiting staff never stay

long, just to check we're busy slaughtering Huns, then back to the Chateau for whisky and soda. Rowlands knows, but it's a good chance to get the trench in shape, train the new boys.

Frog and Pig are paired on the Vickers. Puha is a good hand on the light Lewis. He's half-Maori. He wanted to join their battalion but somebody decided he looked 'too European'. He's got a big grin and one gold tooth — used to be a baker, of all things. Lieutenant Couch, nineteen, is one of those keen sporting types. He thinks the Huns must be barbarians because they don't play rugger.

Rowlands runs our company well, a bit too well sometimes, and we get away with less. There are still casualties. Soames finds a new minefield the hard way and Shaw gets snatched in a trench-raid.

Then a Hun sniper gets busy and two men in C company are shot. So, truce or not, I have to go out with my Mannlicher. The Hun's keen and good but he hasn't been in the front line that long. He can't move as quietly as me and never moves again.

That day, the Hun mortars give us a real plastering. The truce is over and I'm as popular as a dead rat. Rowlands just chuckles, and says any good *Todeshund* would have done the same.

Dog skull

BACK IN THE second trenches, there are always Sunday services. Brasso likes them, because sometimes the Padre hands out sweets and cigs. I went with him once and got bored witless.

I'm Roman Catholic too, whatever that means. Mum was always on her knees or talking to nuns. Roman Catholic, all our street-gang was. Anglicans from the posh boys' school kept away from us. Presbyterians, (press-buttons, we called them), those boys fought us. Being RC mattered a bit in barracks, stopped mattering in the trenches.

At Gallipoli, I met this Turk soldier (another sniper) on a truce-day to bury our dead. Traded him fifty cigs and two cans of bully-beef for a Luger pistol he'd stolen from his officer. He said Christian and Moslem weren't that different — we were 'People of the Book' believing in one God.

Sure, but I got him a week later. I was using a Canadian Ross Mk III then. People of the Book. He had a bullet, 'Faith' scratched on the brass casing. I've got it now.

A chaplain hauls me in to read the lesson — big honour for the fearless sniper; something about the 'Valley of the shadow of death,' could have been written for Flanders. Then we get this sermon about how God is on our side. So what do the Hun padres tell their blokes?

It brings back memories. Our Lady of Fatima on

the corner of old Thorndon Road. Father Thomas, brick-red face and ginger moustaches, crinkly tired blue eyes. His long robe was black with frayed cuffs. It always seemed dark in the church.

Mum was the God-botherer in our family. Always fiddling with the rosary, never did her any damn good. 'God loves and God is always watching,' Father Thomas would say in his creaky voice.

So back in the front lines, we do a listening patrol. On the way back, some Hun pineapples come over and we go flat. Brody, new bloke, ends up with his face in a corpse, gets a mouthful of rotting meat. Now he can't eat, just pukes everything. I wonder if God saw that.

Frog has a theory on this. Frog has a theory on everything. He says since both sides claim God, that God can't be bothered with either. That he's got his feet up in heaven, having a quiet zizz.

The rations are coming around. Stew and dumplings; hard yellow cheese, riddled with fat weevils. I used to spit them out, now I don't bother. They taste like cold jelly. I listen to Brody puking and wonder if Frog is right.

I'm huddled in the remains of a stone fireplace, all that's left of another farmhouse, wondering how stupid the Huns think I am. Jacko Moran the *Todeshund* is supposed to fall for a simple trick — like the one they're trotting out now?

Flies are buzzing and settling around me. I ignore them and look through the telescopic sights of the Mannlicher. In a Hun outpost ahead of me, somebody is bobbing a helmet up and down, the trick we used to flush Dead Willi. But whoever's doing this is as regular as a cuckoo clock.

They really do need to learn some new tricks.

My rifle-barrel scrapes gently on the stonework as I push it forward. A fly settles on the sights. I put my finger to the trigger — time to teach the Hun a trick of my own.

Whoever's bobbing that helmet is just below the parapet. But there's a little crack between two carelessly-stacked sandbags — just inviting a bullet. So I wait till the helmet bobs over it and squeeze the trigger. Phut! The sand scatters, a hole blasted through, the helmet drops.

I think I hit someone and it's time to change position. I'm easing out when hell arrives with a loud scream — a mortar shell exploding, then another — on both sides!

They *do* know some new tricks! I'm running now, never mind the bullets because those bloody mortars have me pegged and the world explodes to hell around me.

I run, I'm thrown over, I run again. I'm knocked

off my feet, shell fragments hiss past like snakes, I should be dead. Behind me the fireplace is blown to rubble. I dive into a crater and huddle in the muddy stink as dirt and unburied body-pieces rain around me. A moment of pause, I swear I can hear the Huns laughing.

That was too damn close. The Huns baited that trap well, the 'regular helmet' and 'chink in the sand-bags' for *Todeshund* to fire at. Bluff and double-bluff. The firing patterns prearranged, with a couple of bracketing shots, then plaster the area — and me.

I'm plastered anyway, in stinking black mud.

They nearly got me that time.

About a week later, Rowlands gets me into the command dugout. Creel is, as usual, away on important duty which usually lasts all day and leaves him stinking of alcohol. Rowlands has been up all night. Looking tired, he's shaving out of a tin cup. He waves me in with his razor. 'We're pulling out day after tomorrow. Get the men ready.'

'Sir.'

Rowlands grunts. 'Only just in time. The bloody lice are eating me alive.'

'Persistent little buggers, sir. Is that all?'

He finishes shaving and wipes his face. 'There is one other item of news. There should be a fanfare with this one, but I couldn't find a trumpet and my gramophone's broken.'

It was actually, when the Huns mortared us.

Rowlands takes out a letter with the War Department crest. Makes to hand it to me, then opens it himself. Maybe he remembered I don't read so well.

He reads it out and it's full of long words like 'unswerving fidelity', 'gallant indifference to his own fate', 'unflinching courage and leadership', 'for all of which displayed by Sergeant Moran, His Majesty is pleased to award the Victoria Cross.'

'The highest award for valour,' says Rowlands softly, 'and you bloody well deserve it.'

He shakes my hand but I still can't take it in. 'Sir, I was doing what I bloody had to. How the hell did I get it?'

'You did more than that.' Rowlands is actually pouring me a drink and smiles. 'But I agree, "how" is the key word.'

He's thinking what I am. Creel would bite off both his arms before writing me up for a decoration. Must have been that toffee-nosed Pom staff officer with all his 'wizards' and 'spiffings'. Because I was making the right noises about King and Country.

He mentions leave and how I might get the medal at the Palace. I still feel gob-smacked, salute and leave. The news is already up the line, courtesy of

Rowlands' blabber-mouth batman, so there's grins and handshakes. I have to grin back and pretend it's normal.

Frog goggles at me with hero-worship, Pig asks me if I'll see the King. Puha says nothing brings the girls running like a medal. Brasso says it'll piss the hell out of Creel.

That at least is good news.

A whole bunch of us went over the Channel for the presentation. It looked good in the papers; the King handing out medals to his brave soldiers in Buckingham Palace. Military Medals, Military Cross, Distinguished Service Order, etc. The other VCs were a couple of Aussies, a Pom airman, a little Gurkha, a tall South African and a Canadian Indian from Vancouver. I paired up with him, Jonas Short-Eagle. He won his cross saving men from a burning ammunition dump.

It was raining in the Channel, and high seas. We nearly collided with a destroyer that came out of nowhere. The crew reckoned they're more trouble than the U-boats — their nickname for Jerry submarines.

This was my second time in England and I thought of Eileen and that cheap trick. I wonder if she's lady's maid by now, on eight bob a week.

It was raining in London too. We got new

uniforms, spit and polish from head to toe. A truck took us to the Palace, where there was a huge mob of people. I've never seen so many red staff tabs together, mostly senior with red boozer faces to match.

I don't remember much, except being sweaty and nervous as hell. Jonas was stiff as a board. The Palace had these big long corridors and red carpet. Huge rooms with gold on the walls and painted ceilings. There was a line of blokes like me, done up in their best, and officers dripping gold braid and brass. And the palace flunkeys, done up like a dog's dinner in wigs and red coats.

Jonas was in front of me, a young airman behind, half his face puckered with burn-scars — he looked about sixteen. And everyone in that big room was looking at us like we're cows for market.

My name was called and I marched up. Remembered the drill by a miracle. The King was like his pictures — bearded, nice smile. He said I was a credit to my country (the whole trench laughed like hell when they read that in the papers) and that our little country was a happy land and an important part of Empire. Sure, I thought, as he pinned the medal on, trade you homes any day. Saluting him, stepping back, the King of England is smiling at Jacko Moran!

Jonas was proud as a peacock. The King had said he was a credit to Canada, a happy land and an important part of Empire. Drinks and sandwiches served, barley-water in little fancy glasses — no booze at the Palace for the duration. We had two days leave and London had a hundred pubs, so we slipped away soon as we could.

Jonas was having his photo taken for the folks and asked did I want to? No, nobody to send it to — then Eileen popped into mind. Wondering *did* she really con me? She was as close as I ever got to a real girlfriend. Maybe she really had a baby and became Mrs Moran, or maybe I just wanted to settle accounts.

'Have you damned colonials forgotten how to salute!' This comes from a purple-faced brigadier with moustache and monocle, the full works. A prune-faced woman in a long fur coat with him looked at us like we were dead rats. The brigadier's pale blue eyes pop angrily.

'I want your names and —'

He breaks off. My unbuttoned greatcoat has flapped open and he sees the purple ribbon and bronze cross. I hear Brit Army rules say that a VC winner gets saluted first — yes, even other ranks — because the officer is saluting the medal.

So we get a frosty glare and his moustache bristles but he does salute, going even redder in the face. We salute back and they go on. His lady looks like she's been dosed with vinegar.

Jonas catches on quick and we hang around the gates, doing that twice more. Staff officers complete with monocle are preferred targets. It's great fun and we're just hitting our stride when an umbrella tip gently taps my shoulder.

'Sergeant.' A sort of gravel voice and deep.

We turn to see a civilian in top hat and frock-coat, smiling. There's authority in his manner, like an officer.

'I cannot salute you, sergeant, being out of uniform. Please accept this with my compliments, for your Crosses.' He slips a big white pound note out of his notecase. 'You've had your fun, now go and enjoy yourselves.'

We grin back and throw him a salute. He raises his top hat.

'Winston Churchill at your service.'

He turns and is lost among the crowds of people coming out. I have the note in my hand then suddenly click who he is. 'Bloody hell, Jonas, know who that was?'

'Who?'

'Winston Churchill, top man at the Admiralty; the bright bugger who dreamed up Gallipoli.' It all looked so bloody simple on paper and I lost most of my best mates there. Jonas gapes as I tear up the pound note and scatter the scraps.

'You mad, Fernleaf?'

''Course I am, I joined the army. Come on, let's find a pub.'

I button my greatcoat as I walk off. I don't want

any more salutes. And I wish I'd clicked to that Churchill name earlier. He wouldn't have got my salute, but he might've got the toe of my boot in memory of good mates.

And in their memory, I got blotto at the nearest pub.

Some time later, Jonas found a woman and I went on to another pub. There was a lot of back-slapping, getting called a 'right blinking hero', while I was buying the drinks. One of them asked if I'd like to meet his sister; meaning he's seen my wad and his sister's for hire. So I mutter something, shoulder out. Walk around the wet streets, manage to hail a cab.

Go back to barracks, I want my head clear for tomorrow.

SHOREDITCH LOOKS just the same, so does the big house where Eileen works. Some kids are trailing after me as I reach the front gate. I stand a minute, thinking. I don't care about that fiver, just want to ask her why. She seemed all right …

I nearly march up to the front door, but I might get it slammed in my face. So I go around the back and knock. I can do a bit of shouting there.

An elderly man answers, wearing one of those fancy vests and pinstriped trousers — a footman I think. There's a fat woman in cook's outfit behind him.

I tell them who I am and ask about Eileen. They look at each other and the man speaks.

Eileen *was* pregnant. And she did go to have her operation, the night before we sailed. She hadn't told anyone else. Apparently something went wrong and the thing was botched. She felt bad on the way home, went into a stonemason's yard to rest. That's where they found her the next morning — sitting against a tombstone of all things.

She'd bled to death.

She wanted better!

The footman tells me this in a queer, grim way. I ask where she's buried, he tells me. Then the woman bursts out, 'Why, want to ask forgiveness for deserting her?'

That's what they think — that I paid her off, dumped her? The door is shut in my face. I want to hammer on it again, to tell them, but what the hell, I do feel to blame. I ask directions to the cemetery and listen to the sound of my boots clopping on the cobble-stoned streets.

I don't like cemeteries, but at least they don't stink of death, like no-man's land. She's in a grave at the back. Her mistress paid for a little headstone. There are withered flowers on it, in a jar. I find some wild marigolds and scatter them over it. I should have done more to stop her. She would have been alive now and would have loved me getting the Cross.

I will make the Huns pay for this!

Then I'm jeering at myself. The Huns didn't give Eileen that fiver. I could have said something — *saved her!* And I'm still standing there when footsteps come up the path behind me.

I turn, a fist hits me —

Four of them and I never find out who they were. That old boy must've phoned someone, other servants, maybe brothers. Anyway it's fists and boots for a few minutes and someone says, 'That's enough, drag the blasted cur away from her grave.'

I'm half-conscious, bleeding, with split lips and a black eye. My ribs are on fire from the boots. With a last kick they throw me over a bench and go.

That's how the cops find me later. Another soldier who made a night of it, got into a scrap. I don't put them wise and don't care about spending the night in the cells.

Next morning an officer appears and tells me the police won't prefer charges but this sort of caper lets the side down, sergeant. Next time the Cross won't save me, so keep your scrapping for the Hun.

And he hopes I enjoyed my leave because it's over.

Fog in the Channel and my thoughts are too black for words. I don't *have* words for the strange feelings I have. The war is awful and the trenches are hell but I belong there. The war made me sergeant and VC winner. It killed Eileen because it brought us together. Mum pushed me under the bed when Dad was drunk, to hide me. Maybe I'm glad to be going back because I can hide in the war.

Foghorns. It's bloody dark and I'm bloody sick.

Victoria Cross

'SARGE, DO YOU know what the bloody Aussies have done now?'

'Shut up, Pig, it's too hot.'

'You know how we're called "Diggers"? Well they're calling themselves that, too.'

'Write to the bloody War Department about it.'

'Muckin' Aussies — they'll pinch anything. It's not right, Sarge.'

'Pig, it doesn't matter.'

'It does. I don't want to be took for no Aussie.'

'You're far too smart and good-looking for that.'

'Yeah? Gee, thanks, sarge. Hey, what're you laughing at, Frog?'

We are entrained and moving to a new sector; a different set of trenches with different rats. We're in boxcars and on flatbeds, on a blazing hot summer's day, and the train's running past a long forest.

There are men in there, and horses, on some kind of exercise. They look spruce and well-fed. We're stopping at a crossroads and shout out to them. Lancers, cavalry, and believe it or not, they still *have* their lances. Hundreds of them, several cavalry regiments, Lieutenant Couch says, Lancers, Hussars, etc, waiting for the breakthrough.

Breakthrough? Turns out the horsemen have been sitting on their backsides for the last three years — on their horses' backsides, rather. Ready to charge through the Hun lines to Berlin — when the poor soddin' infantry have broken the Hun lines.

Puha spits. Has anyone told the cavalry about machine-guns, repeating rifles and bloody cannon? Not to say trenches, minefields and barbed wire?

Couch says the top generals are cavalrymen and have this soft spot, you see. So, at least on the Western Front, they just sit around and watch their horses eat grass.

They were still waiting in 1918.

Spandau machine-gun

I GET A lot of letters about the Cross. And even more crap in papers and journals. Jacko, deadly stalker of Huns, heroic sergeant who turned back a Hun battalion single-handed. The boys love reading them out, until I threaten to shoot the next one I catch. The letters are mainly from schoolgirls and old maids, proposals of marriage and just proposals. But there's also one from younger brother, Georgie.

> DEAR ROBERT, WRITING THIS IN EGYPT, SHOULD
> HAVE DONE IT AT HOME. AM HERE IN THE ARMY,
> THE CAMELS MAKE ME LAUGH. OUR LOT IS COMING
> TO FRANCE, SO WILL SEE YOU. READ A LOT ABOUT
> YOU.
> YOURS, GEORGIE

He's younger than me, with the same black hair, and big like me, too, for his age. Another Moran street-kid, even more light-fingered than me and that's saying something. So he'd be eighteen now. I wonder if Dad got two quid off him too.

We're in the second line, sorting through parcels from home. Most are packed by nice old dears who know as much about the trenches as I do about ballroom dancing. Scarves, socks and pullovers — we always seem to get them in summer. Soap, jars of relish, jam and tea, often broken and mixed together. And fig syrup for 'easy motions'.

'Oh dear,' says Norris, reading out his wife's

letter. 'Butter and cream are hard to get at home and there's no knicker-elastic to be had anywhere. And they're eating rice as a vegetable to save potatoes for our lads in the trenches.'

Our staff in the back lines cop the spuds more likely. I think about Georgie over here. I can put him wise to a few things, lick him into shape.

Pig opens a tin of sardines with a reverent look on his face. Pig would take on the Imperial Hun Guard for sardines. There's some apples — gone rotten, surprise, surprise — and a big fruit cake that Brasso is slicing up with his bayonet. Frog is looking at the papers, wants to be a journalist after the war.

'Sarge,' he asks suddenly, 'do you know a William Moran?'

My father, but screw telling Frog. 'Why?'

'There's a bit here, William Moran, aged 55, fatal accident.'

My shoulders prickle at the memory of his leather belt. I stuff cake in my mouth and take the paper. William Moran, killed when he fell in front of a brewer's dray while intoxicated. Expired before assistance could be summoned.

So the old man's dead. I stuff more cake in my mouth. Pissed as always, seems almost right he was run over by a beer-cart. I still remember his last fond words — *get your mucking head shot off!*

'Related, sarge?' asks Frog, who's been watching

me. So are the others now. I try and swallow the cake but it's too dry.

I take a swig of tea and choke it down, coughing and spraying bits of cake everywhere, and toss the paper back. 'Never knew the bastard.'

The others go back to the boxes. Frog watches a moment longer until I eyeline him, then goes back to his paper. It's no more than the truth, I never did know him and it's too late now.

Georgie would've sailed before it happened. I'll have to tell him, but I don't expect tears.

Four a.m. We are waiting for the Mad Minute.

The firing step is manned, no smoking and complete silence. The metal of our weapons is ice-cold. It's cold-range work so I've put away my Mannlicher for an Enfield. Morning dew drips off the rim of my helmet.

The Huns intend a local attack on this trench-line. There's a new battalion opposite and some German general has decided they need 'blooding'. *Hun generals love that word too.* It means a lot of men will be killed so the survivors get some real battle experience.

They cut the wire last night. There will be no bombardment. Things have been quiet and they hope to take us by surprise.

Some hope. A deserter comes over, a scruffy

little peace-time railway porter who doesn't like life in the glorious German Army. Says his sergeant had it in for him. I would like to boot him back and, I think, so would Rowlands, but HQ want him so he's carefully escorted down the line.

A lot of his mates will die, but his hide is safe.

Dawn. Our frozen breath is in puffy clouds as we wait for the Mad Minute. Rowlands looks over, from the trench periscope.

'Coming.'

'Click' as the hammer of his Webley revolver goes back and the clickety-click-click of the rifle-bolts. Beside me, Frog pulls back the cocking lever of the Vickers, a small tinkle as Pig readies the cartridge belts.

Do I want to do this? *Why even think that?* I've done it so many times; kill your enemy before he kills you. Months and months in stinking trenches like this, feet frozen, gut wrenching. The rifle's cold on my unshaven cheek, the lice are crawling in my groin, itching like hell.

I am bloody sick of this!

Click-click again. Rowlands loads a flare pistol and points it skyward. Here it comes, you poor buggers, let's hope just once, your general has enough sense to order recall.

Up sails the flare and bursts a deep burning red.

A crash thunders around us and my rifle jars my shoulder … the sweetish smell of cordite. More flares, the German troops running towards us, rifles high like bloody drill. The Mad Minute has begun. Like always, I hear my drill instructor's yell.

Like riding a bike, lads, never forget!

Mad Minute, trained to fire fast as we can, fifteen rounds a minute, then another mad minute and another because the Germans keeping coming. We are firing fast, the loud constant din is nearly drowning out the stutter of the Vickers.

The old bugger could've stayed alive long enough to see my medal. Rage building again, choking and strong — *I made something of myself.* Scrambling up onto the parapet, legs astride the sandbags; working the Enfield like me and the rifle are one machine.

Want to see a real Mad Minute?

Steady press of the trigger, the butt kicks to my shoulder, at the same moment I flick open the bolt. With my left wrist I tilt the rifle right to eject the cartridge clear, then push the bolt-knob up, back, and forward again with the next round. Take first pressure as foresight lines with backsight, squeeze trigger, butt thumps shoulder, open bolt again — *like riding a bike*.

In the crashing din around me, no pause when I fire the last shot, hand to the pile of full clips, grab the bolt, thumb-pressure to force the bullets out of the clip into the empty magazine, bolt home, aim, five more thumps against my shoulder. I hear Rowlands yelling, 'Get down!' *Screw you!*

Then it's over. Ten mad minutes, a few hundred thousand rounds at maybe a thousand troops. There are grey bundles huddled everywhere now, some on the uncut wire, some writhing and screaming. One such bundle only twenty yards from our trench, upturned helmet beside it. So they got close enough. I slip back down.

We wait but they don't come again. Maybe the generals have decided they're blooded enough. Rowlands is at the trench periscope again. 'About three hundred dead,' he mutters.

Once we would have shouted; these days, we just nod and keep alert. Our artillery opens up and the Hun 5.9s reply. Rowlands comes over to me.

'Sergeant, there's an expression, "taking the pitcher to the well". It means that sooner or later the law of averages catches up with you. Next time, do as you're bloody told.'

The law of averages? More like a Mauser bullet. I nod with a 'Yes, sir,' and we both know damn well I don't mean it. He holsters his revolver and moves off down.

Pig pushes back his helmet and has a look through the periscope. 'Geez,' he mutters. 'Too damn easy.'

Pitcher to the well.

There's this time outside Pozières. We are working across a field, muddy and shell-cratered. The Huns have a pillbox sited here nicknamed 'Bowler' because it's round like the hats.

Bowler is a hard nut to crack. There are infantry and field-guns behind it so we go to earth. Rowlands sends back a runner for artillery support and we are told to wait. An hour passes, Bowler spits out endless bullets.

Then we hear a growling sound like nothing I've ever heard before. We look over, and nosing across the mud come two big steel things. Steel-plated like huge armoured slugs, grinding along on linked-steel tracks. A gun, six-pounder, sticking out either side.

'What the blue blazes …?' breathes Rowlands.

Tanks. The first we've seen. One slows, the hatch opens, an officer pops his head out. Helmet and chain-mail mesh over his face against bullets splattering against the vision-slits. He just grins when we point out Bowler.

'Soon have them cleaned up,' he says with a cheerful wave.

We've heard a lot about tanks. They're supposed to win the war for us but, judging from these two, we'll have a long wait. As they roll forward, one runs over a mine, a track comes undone and it's finished. The second manages one shot against Bowler (bouncing off the reinforced concrete) then gets hit by a Hun shell.

The survivors double back amid bullets, a lot faster than they went out. The Hun artillery pounds both tanks into scrap metal. So the attack on Bowler fails and we fall back. There are some good men dead, Lofty among them. The tanks burn into the night.

'Whose bright ideas were those, sir?' I ask Rowlands.

'Former First Sea Lord, Winston Churchill.'

'The same Winston Churchill who said Gallipoli would knock the Turks out of the war?'

'I believe so,' Rowlands is trying to eat an army biscuit. He'd have better luck with a slab of concrete. 'He says they will revolutionise the face of battle. Win the war.'

Oh sure they will. But only if the Germans die laughing.

Black September ... Not for us but for the Air Force. We're used to the crazy little bi-planes circling overhead and shooting at each other, the bigger bombers that go over to hit the Hun rear depots, and the older planes that just circle and call in artillery strikes on the ground.

We have anti-aircraft guns, nicknamed 'ack-ack'. Ours fire shells that explode in white smoke; the German shells explode in black smoke, both drifting in the blue sky. We ignore planes now, unless they get personal and try to bomb us, or if they crash in the lines.

It's called 'Black September' because trench rumour says we are losing the air war. The Hun aircraft are better and faster, three-winged ones called 'tri-planes' and one called an 'Albatross', two-winged and like a big shark. They're all colours, black, white, green and purple, red; yellow, orange and red, checks, stripes, zig-zags.

The German aircraft paraded themselves like they were the best — and they were — shooting our boys out of the sky.

Anyway, one of ours, a two-seater Bristol some-thing, comes down, a bright red tri-plane right on his arse. The Bristol crash-lands in no-man's land and the tri-plane swoops up again. The pilot gets out; his gunner, riddled with bullets, doesn't.

Rowlands yells for covering fire and, by a miracle, the pilot makes it to our trench, does a header inside. Rowlands fills him with tea and we con-tact his airfield. Then I take him down to the second line, to wait for transport.

He says he's seventeen; but the Air Force isn't fussy about age, either. He's been combat flying for a week and the six pilots who joined with him are already shot down — 'gone west'. And the red tri-plane ('Tripehound' he nicknames it) that shot him down, is flown by the 'Red Baron' himself, the top Hun ace.

We chat about gunnery (ground-to-air) and I ask about those new escape-things the Huns use now to get out of the crashing aircraft. He supplies the word — parachutes. And shakes his head — not allowed on our side. The generals (who don't fly) think they'll help cowards dodge action.

He's all right for an officer — young, looks twitchy, strained as hell. Even his jokes are nervous. He shakes my hand when the car arrives, and goes — of course I never see him again.

Our artillery smashes the crashed aircraft into matchwood because we don't want the Huns removing anything. It burns in a few minutes.

Sooner him than me, five thousand feet up, in a wood-and-canvas crate held together with wire and glue.

Rowlands says new pilots last about ten hours' flying time.

'So what d'you think'll happen now the Ruskis are shooting each other?' says Brasso.

Him, me, Puha and a new bloke, Randall, are in a forward post. Night, and the Hun is playing games. Shooting up a mix of red, blue and green flares then dropping pineapples up and down the line. Not clever to announce themselves like this? But sometimes the Hun is too bloody clever, so we stay tense.

'Never mind the bloody Russians!' I whisper.

'If they drop out of the war, we're stuffed,' says Puha.

'Open your gob once more and you're stuffed anyway,' I whisper.

The Russian Army has collapsed; just folded up and gone home. A 'People's Government' whatever that is, has taken over. Their King — Czar they call him — has been kicked off his throne; rumour is he's already copped a bullet.

Another flare hisses up and glows a deep horrible red on our faces as we look up. It takes forever to drop down. Maybe they've picked up one of our patrols in no-man's land, or maybe they're lighting one of theirs home.

More pineapples whistle over and A Company trenches cop it this time.

'So the Hun armies on the Eastern Front will come over here,' whispers Brasso, taking this as an excuse to start talking again. 'Maybe we should go home too, eh?'

'The French tried that,' says Puha.

Another flare goes up. Green this time. I use the light to grab Puha by his neck and shake him a little. Just so that he gets the message. Brasso gets a kick. *Shut it!*

The French did try it. Their whole damn army mutinied and if Jerry found out, the Kaiser'd be in

Buckingham Palace by now. So the French High Command got together a few hundred of the ringleaders in a field for 'talks'. But they did the talking with a box-barrage of 75mm artillery fire; result, craters and bits of bodies.

End of mutiny.

Another set of mortar bombs fall downline. Something is wrong. I prop the light Lewis up on the sandbags, Brasso gets the hint and cocks his Enfield. So do the others, Randall a little nervous but ready.

Another flare bursts, blue again.

Still that gut feeling, something is wrong.

Tense, thinking about what Brasso said. If the Russians have folded, that's maybe another thirty Hun divisions freed up for the Western Front. We can't match that manpower or even come close to it.

No mortars but another flare — yellow this time.

Yellow! And dropping right over our trench, lighting us up.

Hell! I shout to the others, grab the flare pistol and fire it up, shouldering the light Lewis as our white flare bursts overhead.

There they are — looming out of the dark, those spiked helmets. The Lewis gun jars on my shoulder and spits loudly, the ammo drum turning in tiny clicks. They are caught in our flare, Lewis and Enfield bullets knocking them over. A hoarse shout and one arm going up, throwing something.

'Bomb!' I shout.

It explodes on the trenchline, sandbags blown into the air. A yell of pain beside me. I keep firing, Brasso and Pig work their Enfields, as fast as they can. The rest of the trench is coming to life and the German raiding party — those left alive — withdraw.

It was clever. The mortar-fire and flares to keep us guessing all up and down the line. Yellow, the colour to attack. A snatch patrol, probably after prisoners — imagine their delight at getting *Todeshund*.

So we can breathe again, but there's still a lot of racket, both sides hammering away. We pull back and another party mans the outpost. Randall has a bomb fragment in his arm — and proud of it!

'I can write to the folks about this,' he gasps, like he's got a medal. 'They'll know I'm in the thick of it.'

'It's a scratch mate, not a ticket home,' says Pig, puzzled, wrapping on a field dressing.

'A wound of honour,' Randall winces. 'Anyway, I'd rather be with my comrades.'

I tell Pig to get him down to the first-aid station. Brasso and me look at each other. Wound of honour? I thought like that once. Got my leg nicked in Gallipoli and scared as hell it would take me out of the trenches.

Wound of honour. What the hell was that?

I MAKE A report to Captain Rowlands. He smiles a little when I tell him what Randall said and tells me to help myself to tea.

'Honour?' Then, 'I got stuck in a stores job at Anzac Cove. I hated it, felt I was practically dodging duty. I met your old platoon sergeant there, Harry Wainwright.'

Jessica Collingwood's boyfriend. He was a good soldier and Creel sent him on a useless patrol. Harry was shot in the stomach, died a few hours later, and I told Creel what I thought of him. Rowlands must know this by now.

'I knew Harry from school,' says Rowlands. 'He was a year older than me but hell, what a change.' He sips his tea. 'If I met Rowlands from Lemnos today, I wouldn't know him.'

Rowlands is all right, shares a joke but always keeps the distance. It's not like him to talk personally.

'1918 soon,' Rowlands says. He's got a sharp face, a little moustache and untidy brown hair, with wrinkled green-brown eyes. 'And there's no bloody end in sight, Moran. I shouldn't be saying that, but it's true.'

'Are the Russians really broken, sir?'

Rowlands nods. 'In the words of their new leader, a chap called Lenin, the Russian Army has voted with its feet. So a lot of Hun divisions are coming our way. Battle troops, not conscripts.'

'We've got the Yanks coming, sir.'

'Yes.' He sloshes his tea around, sips it. 'So maybe even bigger battles and a lot more dead.' He looks at me. 'What'll it mean to you, sergeant?'

'I'll be twenty, sir.' Just that, because nothing else will change. I see his slightly puzzled look and explain. 'Joined when I was seventeen, sir. Big for my age.'

Some of the men are singing down the trench now, a new song going the rounds.

'There's a long, long trail awinding, into the land of my dreams …'

I yell for them to shut up. The Huns can zero a mortar on that noise. Rowlands is speaking.

'I joined because it was the right thing to do. Duty to Empire, God, King and Country. Fighting the war to end all wars.'

I decide to be honest. 'For regular pay, decent clothes and a new pair of boots.'

He just smiles. 'And you're a natural fighter, a damn good soldier. You could get a field commission for the asking. A few weeks' training and come back an officer.'

Me? No more sniping, getting drunk with the lads, the thought hits my guts like a Hun bullet. A mucking officer! I say, 'No!' so quickly that I forget to add 'sir'.

Rowlands just smiles, I think it's the answer he expected. 'All right, sergeant. Dismissed.'

Outside his dugout in the cold night air, it comes to me. Sergeant Moran, as far as I'll go in the army. And I know damn well there'll be no room for Sergeant Moran in peacetime. But peacetime is a bloody hundred years away and I might be dead tomorrow. Because this war doesn't end and doesn't change.

1918. More of the same.

Mannlicher

New Zealand, 1940

IT'S NEAR *dawn now. I always know when it's dawn, every soldier does. You wake then, see, because that's when the Hun pays a call. Even in the work camp I woke at dawn.* Sweating — those bloody nightmares, mud, rotting bodies. *I could drown them in alcohol but, like bloated corpses, they always surfaced again.*

Huns ... corpses ... hospital windows, long and narrow, covered with dark grey curtains. I can just see them but the dawn shadows are very dark, maybe send up a flare — the Hun —

'Don't mind the shadows, Jacko ...'

What the hell does Jessica Collingwood see in me? Did I remind her of Gallipoli and Harry — she never stopped loving him. But she wasn't there then, when I was back in the war. I wonder why Harry hasn't come, or Hooter, O'Donnell, Tiny, Gallipoli mate who —

'You'll see them all again soon, Jacko. Soon.'

Her hand is on my forehead.

Yes, going over the top soon, a last cigarette in cupped hands, frost on the bloody sandbags, the stink is never frozen —

There's a scratchy raspy sound like sandpaper on wood. My breathing, no pain; just the awful awkward labour of dragging air into my lungs.

Put your bloody mask on —

Waited a bit long, eh? Sure, I saved the others and the war was ending. War, the only thing I was good at. I was good at war. I'm no good at dying.

Kitchener poster

Flanders, 1918

The hell where youth and laughter go ...

— 'Suicide in the Trenches', Siegfried Sassoon

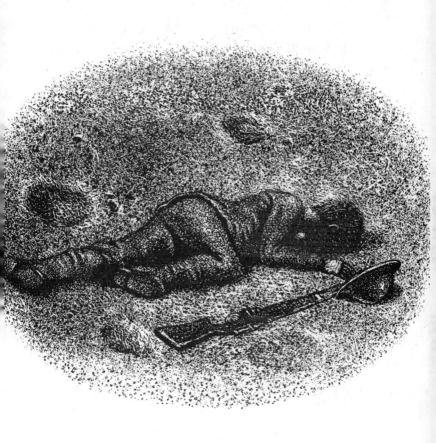

'HERE THEY COME,' mutters Brasso. 'I'm bloody looking forward to this.'

'Yeah, sod him,' says Pig.

He spits as the party comes into sight. A few 77s coming over from the Hun lines, otherwise quiet, but won't stay like that. The Huns have been shelling all morning, so a lot of damned spade-work tonight to repair the damage. That doesn't put us in a good mood, either.

'Sergeant!' shouts Creel.

This must be important if that yellow-livered red-faced pig is risking his hide. I learn later that battalion orders specified he do the job; so maybe they're wise to him at last. He's sweating, nervous, whisky on his breath. He ducks, as a shell screams overhead, and jabs a thumb.

'Get on with it.'

'Sir.'

The man is held between two soldiers but not struggling. He's tall, pale-faced, with deep-set eyes and his chin is covered with dark stubble. He lets them push him to the ground and strap his arms to the framework of poles. He looks up at the sky, clouds and shell-smoke overhead. If he's scared, he doesn't show it.

'Get him up,' orders Creel.

Rowlands is there, saying nothing. Brasso and I, Pig at the back, push the framework up so the man is over the trenchline; in full view of the Hun. A sitting target for bullets or shells.

'Just say the right word, you bloody conchie,' yells Creel, 'and you're down again.' Creel's not enjoying this. Oh, shoving a conchie at the Germans is all right but a bullet might miss and hit *him*.

The conchie has said nothing, hanging limp in the straps. Brasso has bet he'll last five minutes; he loses his bet. The man's eyes seem unfocused, as though he's seeing things we can't. Some Hun bullets ping around him then stop — they won't do our dirty work for us.

The Hun artillery can't see him though, and the shells continue to scream over. Ten minutes go by, half an hour. Creel is chalky white now and our conscientious objector to military service just hangs limp as the shrapnel peppers around him. He's untouched and unmoving, his eyes half-closed as though none of this matters.

I take a swig from my canteen, starting not to like this. OK, the bugger doesn't want to fight. But he's no coward, standing up to it better than Creel.

'All right,' says Creel, trying not to let his voice squeak. 'Get him down, put him up again after an hour.' We drop the conchie back into the trench. 'This is what brave men face all the time, you stinking coward.'

Even Rowlands blinks at that one. And I don't like any bugger who won't fight — but *Creel*, the yellow maggot himself? He stalks off towards the communication trench that leads to the rear.

'Untie him,' orders Rowlands.

We do so and pull the conchie up. He looks around like he's woken up from a dream. I've heard some of the other things the army does to them. Maybe he's learned just to shut off. He's pushed down to sit on the firing step.

'You do have courage,' says Rowlands.

The conchie looks at him blankly then shrugs. A big drum of tea is being lugged along the trench. Frog takes a mouthful of his, hesitates, takes it to the conchie.

'Hey!' shouts Pig, outraged

'Go on,' says Rowlands.

He drinks it in several gulps like he's parched. Frog gives him some hard-tack and cheese, which he scoffs like he hasn't eaten for a week. His hands are shaking now and there's something in his eyes. Maybe the food has reminded him he's still alive.

There's a lull in the shelling — maybe the Huns have knocked off for a cup of their acorn-coffee. More like to refill their ammo wagons. Rowlands goes over to the conchie, sitting huddled and silent.

'Baxter,' he says, 'you can face that, so you can face anything. Why not do as the army wants?'

Baxter rubs a hand over his stubbled mouth. He blinks and swallows, like it's an effort to speak. 'They want too much,' he says.

Rowlands is patient. 'You could drive an ambulance. Even do rear-echelon work. They just want you to submit.'

'That is too much,' he replies.

Rowlands gives up. A few minutes pass and the MP sergeant checks his watch. Looks at Rowlands, indicates the framework.

'Up again, sir?'

Rowlands seems about to nod. Then says, 'Read your orders, sergeant. Punishment under supervision of Major Creel. Do you see him anywhere?'

'Sir —'

'When he returns, sergeant. Not until then.'

Of course Creel doesn't return; this is later explained as a mix-up in orders. So the conchie sits there while the German shellfire starts again; shrapnel shreds the sandbags around him. He's still unmoving, still unmarked.

'Not a scratch,' mutters Brasso. 'No bloody justice, eh?'

This time though, he doesn't get a murmur of agreement.

Even Pig is silent.

Nobody likes to see the rat Creel calling anyone else a coward, and that guy took his punishment without squealing. Evening comes and no Creel, so he's packed off again. We never find out what happened to him.

So we fall to and repair the damage; refill sandbags, restack them on the parapet. Dig out a couple of shelters that have collapsed. Meanwhile the Hun machine-guns make life as difficult as they can. The conchie's framework is chopped up for firewood

Some time in the dark, Rowlands calls me over. The trenchline is patched up and he wants a patrol out to check a new Hun observation post. Of course, Sergeant Moran will lead it. I nod then think of something. 'Sir, what'd that beggar mean? Submitting was too much?'

'His principles allowed no compromise. Jesus Christ said more or less the same thing to the Romans.'

I'm not a religious man but that doesn't make sense. 'Sir, what's a sodding conchie got to do with Jesus?'

Rowlands shrugs. 'God knows, sergeant. Carry on.'

Brasso has overheard this. He makes a spitting noise through his lips. 'Then God should explain it to us,' he mutters.

This time there *is* a murmur of agreement, but nobody talks about the 'yellow' conchie again. And he's even got me wondering what fear is. Or courage.

God knows.

Lee Enfield and Mauser rifles

'IT'S QUIET over there,' says Rowlands. 'Too bloody quiet.'

He's looking intently through a trench periscope. I'm looking through another, and he's right. No cooking-fire smoke, no noise and unseen bustle. No rifle or machine-gun fire — no mortars.

Nothing.

'Ah. They're just laying for us,' says Pig.

'All at once you're a soddin' expert?' I growl.

Pig takes the hint and shuts up. But it *is* too quiet — come to think of it, it's been quiet for a week. A few patrols, the odd mortar session — even Parapet Joe seems to have lost his touch.

This is different though. This is silence.

We jump as the telephone jangles in Rowlands' dugout. Lieutenant Couch answers it, listens and hangs up. He comes up to Rowlands.

'Major Creel, sir, HQ. A patrol to look at the Hun lines.'

'In broad daylight?' That is plain bloody stupid and Rowlands' tone says so.

'Yes, sir. Says things are like this all along the Front.'

Rowlands sighs. 'All right. Sergeant, get a patrol together. Eight men.'

'Shall we wait for Major Creel, sir?'

'Get bloody moving.'

We assemble. The light Lewis gun in Frog's

capable hands, Pig with the spare ammo drums. Brasso, who can chuck a bomb with the best of them, Randall and a couple of others — Rowlands and Couch.

Silence.

We move out. We keep low, in among the shell-craters and the muddy water — always there, even in summer. The mud is hard, frozen patches, and there's a pale January sun overhead.

Ahead is only the silence.

It's not real, I tell myself. This is a Hun trick, it must be. They are waiting, they're good soldiers, the best; they don't just pack up and go. They're this quiet for one reason only.

To kill us.

Up and down the line, other patrols are moving forward. Because the Hun lines are quiet everywhere. And yes, they might be waiting for us and they'd kill a few — but is it worth all this? Shelling would account for more. So we're halfway across now and —

Flutter — shit, what was that!

A bird, a lark I think, zooming skyward. Birds have no business in no-man's land. Even with wings, they can't beat the flying lead. We see crows some-times, bound to with all the dead meat.

So what is a lark doing here?

The flies buzz around my nose; the mud is nearly solid. I am leading the way because I know this trenchline. There, where I shot the soldier wire-cutting; now bellying into the crater where I shot that Hun officer, his fancy helmet too bright for his own good. My eyes slit as I inch my head over the crater rim.

Ahead is the Hun front line.

I was close then, too bloody close. The Hun officer was a tempting target. Now I am looking at just the same line of sandbags.

Nothing moves. Silence.

'Anything?' comes Rowlands' whisper from behind.

'Nothing.'

And 'nothing' is right. Because in front of me is a narrow dark slit in the parapet sandbags. Just wide enough for a Spandau barrel to traverse.

There is another about twenty yards down; just the dark slit and no machine-gun. Another bird, a sparrow, flies down to perch on the sandbags. No smell of cooking fires, no noise at all.

Something is bloody wrong!

Rowlands has bellied up beside me. He raises his binoculars. This is the moment any Hun marksman has been waiting for; sunlight flashing on the binoculars like a pointing finger. Rowlands is dead, I wait for the shot.

He lowers the binoculars. Mutters, his lips touching the mud. 'Sergeant, do you know your Sherlock Holmes?'

Sherlock Holmes? Am I supposed to have heard of someone with a bloody stupid name like that? There are ways of telling officers when they ask stupid questions. Even when you're waiting to get blown up.

'Was he a Hun general, sir?'

Rowlands gets the message, nods and smiles. Spits black mud from his lips before replying. 'Sherlock Holmes was a fictional Victorian detective. Absolute master at solving mysteries. And he had this favourite saying …'

The January sun seems hotter, on the silent Hun trenchline, with the flies buzzing. I am sweating because this is all wrong, just too bloody quiet and strange.

'He said,' goes on Rowlands, 'that when all other explanations are eliminated, whatever remains, however impossible, must be the truth.'

What is this, a soddin' comic turn?

He looks at me. 'And the truth is, the Huns aren't there.'

Oh sure, very clever, Mr Rowlands. Did you work that out all by yourself? Well, fine, I was thinking the same. Pity Mr Sherlock Holmes's not here, he could stroll across to the Hun trench and see for himself.

A clatter — Rowlands stands.

I yell and grab at him but he's stepping forward. He walks up to the Hun parapet; for sheer cold nerve I have never seen anything like it. And since he's such a bloody brave officer, I have to be a bloody brave sergeant. I stand too, a little gut-wrench inside, expecting the bullets to slam me back into the mud.

Nothing. I take a step forward. Then another and another.

Rowlands is already at the trenchline, looking up and down. Now the Hun bullets should be spinning him around. Instead, he jumps so quickly out of sight that I have to run and jump down beside him.

I land on German duckboards, as muddy and slippery as our own; near as hell turn my ankle. The patrol follows, Brasso landing beside me, skidding and ending up on his backside. He curses loud enough for the Kaiser in Berlin to hear.

'Shut up!' I whisper, but still my voice is the only sound. Pig clatters over; he never does anything quietly. Frog comes up with the Lewis gun, the others behind him. The duckboards squish gently underneath.

Silence.

We are in the Hun front lines, usually just a collection of fortified trench-holes and linking trenches. Ahead, though, is a communications trench. Rowlands, revolver in hand, goes down it and we follow.

The second trenchline opens up. It's as deep as ours, sandbagged, and the entrances to those deep concrete bunkers of theirs are carefully sited and well-built by troops who've had little else to do these three years. Rowlands stops at a bunker door, made of solid planks. It's swinging ajar.

'Sergeant.'

I know what to do, signal Brasso to take the other side. Pull out the Mills-bomb pin as he kicks the door in. Throw in and huddle back as it explodes, banging the door out again.

Silence.

Inside, the dugout is torn apart. But even looking around, I can see the place has been abandoned. Four Huns lived here. There are some old tins and empty bottles, a candle-stump and a torn blanket, but nothing personal. No photos, food or clothes. So maybe Rowlands and Sherlock are right.

Whatever remains … however impossible …

We kick open the next door. I go in with my bayonet out, looking for tripwires and boobytraps because the Huns know as many tricks as old Sherlock. But it's all the same — possessions gone, like they just took off.

The trench is quiet, hot, the flies buzzing. We check another door and my flesh creeps in tiny cold prickles. I don't believe in ghosts but we all know about the Angel of Mons. Looking into these silent dugouts brings it back — the time when the Germans nearly broke the British Army on the Marne River.

When they attacked, they were beaten back — by

a miracle, some said. The miracle was the 'Mad Minute', rifle-fire so intense that the Huns thought they were walking into massed machine-guns. It was such an impossible victory that rumours started.

Rumours of an angel-figure, Saint George in silver armour with his dazzling lance. Another version is of massed bowmen from the old days when English arrows turned back the French knights. Stories. But the padres are always saying God is on our side. Standing in those dark dugouts, the stories seemed more real. The morning sunlight was better. Rowlands has gone up the trench and returns, holstering his pistol. He stops and looks around.

'The Huns have bloody well hooked it. To parts unknown.'

'Sir?' Good news or bad always makes Pig frown because he has to think. 'How can they just go like that?'

'No idea, private. They forgot to ask my permission.'

Now a runner comes scrambling down the trenchline from A Company's patrol; then one up from C Company. All along the lines, the Huns have pulled back to Lord knows where.

Rowlands lights a cigarette. 'Wherever, I bet it's bad news for us.'

Pig drops the bag of ammo drums and they clatter in the stillness. 'Maybe they've gone home to Berlin.'

Pig thinks all the Germans live in Berlin. Rowlands shakes his head, I can see he's still worried. I am too. It's strange just being here. We are still walking down the trenches, deep-firing positions, well-made firing steps, a binocular case lying on the duckboards.

'Mine!' shouts Randall and runs up.

'Randall!' I shout, just ahead of Rowlands.

The explosion slams Randall against the trench wall. His body slides down with a thump. He's dead.

'I should've warned him!' says Rowlands bitterly.

You can't always out-think the Hun. They'd leave some areas free, others booby-trapped to hell. A mine under a duckboard, maybe the next door we push open, under a rude postcard, as one bloke from C Company finds out. Delayed-action explosives in a bunker. Six men buried when that goes up.

THEY HAD pulled back a bit, leaving the booby-traps like a tart's farewell kiss.

Now they had a new line, a few miles back; twice as strong as the one they had just left. Better trenches, concrete pill-boxes and underground bunkers three storeys deep. All the damned barb-wire in the world, and strongpoints with names like Siegfried, and Wotan, etc. Legendary German heroes, says Rowlands.

And those few miles they pulled back wiped out all our gains; all the quarter-million men who died in the mud to make them. They called this the Hindenburg Line and were now waiting behind it, waiting for all those divisions from the Eastern Front. So three years of bloody fighting go for bloody nothing.

Yes, 1918 would be more of the same.

Spandau machine-gun

WE DON'T GET a close look at the Hindenburg Line just then. We're pulled out to rest camp and march down one of those *pavé* roads again. It's raining, with a cold wind blowing, but with a rest-camp ahead nobody cares.

I remember the first time we marched down a French road. Sun, heat and dust then, a whole sodding lifetime ago. Then we sang 'Run, Rabbit, Run' and 'Mademoiselle from Armentières'. Today's song is different.

> *'We're here because we're here,*
> *because we're here, because we're here,*
> *We're here because we're here ...'*

It's not even sung really. Just a cross between a growl and a moan. The sole of my boot is flapping, the lice are driving me mad and the wet mud clogs my uniform. My pack is sodden, seems twice as heavy. Ten of those French kilometres to go.

'We're here, because we're here, because —'

Ahead, we can hear another sound: officers on horseback coming out of the misting rain, a column of men behind them. They are singing too, but cheerfully as though bloody enjoying themselves.

'Cripes,' says Brasso, 'real singing? Don't tell me they've emptied the loony bins.'

The British are conscripting old men, sick men and under-age boys. Any one-eyed, knock-kneed half-wit who can hold a rifle.

This is 1918 and nobody sings on their way to the front. They must have a skinful of rum I think, then I hear the song they are singing and it makes sense.

Over there, over there,
Send the word, send the word, over there,
That the Yanks are coming, the Yanks are coming,
The drums rum-tumming —

'Hey, it's Yanks!' shouts Pig.

There've been rumours that a hundred thousand American troops have landed already, and four hundred thousand more are on the way, but these are the first we've seen and our line shambles to a stop, much to Creel's fury. We wait and cheer as they come up.

Their officers salute with their swords. Then the troops march by, the same tin helmets as us, big packs, new raincoats and strong boots. Good men with sun-burned faces and the new Springfield rifles. The mud splashes under their tramping boots and the line seems to go on forever.

Lord knows what they think of the muddy tramps cheering at them. In a week they'll look like us. Right now they grin and toss fags over — even candy. 'You Tommies sure are a bunch of mud-hogs,' one calls.

'Mud-hogs' is all right but not 'Tommies'. We make allowances though, because we're so damned pleased to see them. We shoulder arms again and keep marching. There must be a couple of thousand of them, big, fit men, looking full of fight. Thank God they were smart enough not to let the Poms use them as cannon-fodder. Then they pass on, a line of honking trucks following.

Pig scowls at a piece of candy. 'Chewing gum?' he says. 'What'd you do with it?'

'Chew it,' says Frog. 'Don't swallow.'

Pig chews it for half an hour then complains the taste has gone. So what should he do now? Frog tells him (except he uses the word 'backside') and nearly starts a fight.

The war is getting to us all. Frog never used to say things like that.

In rest camp for two whole weeks. We strip off our filthy rags, have a really hot shower, with rough cakes of yellow army soap and our bodies red with lice-bites. Then a big hot meal of stew and a full night's sleep. No sentries. As close to normal as it gets in the army.

There were canteens with old ladies dishing out tea and biscuits. Religious services but I stay away from them. Mum was always on her knees but it did her no damn good. We can eat army food or stroll to a little nearby town; get egg and chips for a franc, then go on to an *estaminet*.

There are soldiers here from everywhere. French African troops in their funny red caps, Aussies, Canadians, Japanese; some soldiers with a type of dustbin-lid helmet — Portuguese I think. Sikhs in turbans, Indians, who are pulling out for Egypt soon. The local girls say they're polite, clean and well-mannered — unlike us. Cheeky bitches.

A lot of local girls and older women. Painted up and stinking of cheap perfume. Most in a place called the Black Lily. They know just enough English, always have their hand out for the money.

Creel's nowhere to be seen as usual. Word is he's after a staff job, well back of the lines. Greasing enough to fry a side of bacon, I'll bet.

Brasso gets a poker session going and cleans out some Irish fusiliers. Then gets cleaned out himself by a couple of smiling Sikhs and a West African lorry driver. Pig said he shouldn't let himself get beaten by native troops and Brasso's reply starts them fighting.

We all joined in, till the MPs got stuck into us with batons. Like old times in Holloway Road with the cops.

We can still hear the guns though and sometimes the night sky is red, like a fire being stoked. We get drunk, look for a woman — do all the things not to think about the fire. We'll go back soon enough.

Mail catches up with me, a letter from Georgie.

DEAR ROBERT, WE'RE IN PLACE CALLED SHORED-ITCH, NOT BAD BUT THE BEER IS WARM. WE'RE DOING A LOT OF LIVE-AMMO FIRING. THE WORD IS WE'LL COME OVER TO FRANCE SOON. SEE YOU THEN, GEORGIE.

Funny, but it's hard to remember him. He was thin — that happens when your dad takes the food-money for drink. Georgie had freckles, long untidy hair, a big grin. Always messy, but the army would take care of that.

Somebody gets up a set of Empire Rugby Matches. I'm fly-half for our team, snipers can move fast. We beat the Welsh, then the Scots, collect a few black eyes and bruises. Then the Ghurkhas, little Nepalese blokes who don't like losing. They scamper off with loud angry mutters.

Their officer comes over. He's got long fair moustaches, a very tidy uniform and a riding-crop. He politely asks Rowlands if 'we chaps' know much about Ghurkha honour? Says the little chaps don't like losing and have gone to get their Kukri knives. They can take a chap's head right off with those, don't you know, old chap?

So it might be an idea, he says, for our chaps not to hang around. Or there might be a spot of bloodshed when his chaps get back. Rowlands thinks the officer-chap is pulling our legs. But we were leaving anyway and even Pig manages a fair speed.

George is coming. It'll be good to see him again.

A good rest camp, even with the fights. Even film shows. But that's not why I remember it. I met some-one I'd nearly forgotten.

Jessica Collingwood.

It was two days before we went back up the lines. Now it was more than a rumour: the Russians wanted an armistice and were starting their own civil war.

So with them out, the German Army fighting them would join the German Army fighting us. That stacked up to a lot of battle-tough divisions coming our way.

And we were really scraping the bottom of the bucket. All the Brits could manage now were green conscripts, pimply kids and former rejects not even sure which end of the rifle to use. All their good men used up at Somme, Passchendaele and the others. This lot would run if the Hun just farted.

Of course a Yank army was on the way. Fresh

bright young blokes and full of fight, like those first Brit divisions. But the Germans knew that and as Rowlands put it — would they be obliging enough to wait?

I had a queer sense about this spell of the line — felt like it would be the last for a long time. The Germans wouldn't stay put behind their great Hindenburg forts. All the damned army knew that — except the generals.

We'd win or the Germans would — either way there'd be peace and if I was still alive, I'd go home. Home. What the hell was that?

I WANDERED DOWN to the town that evening for an egg and chips. I had two lots, served by a nice giggling waitress. She's the owner's daughter though, and he's built like a bloody truck, a big kitchen-cleaver stuck in his belt. He slaps it and I get the message. There's a nice picture of the Virgin Mary on the wall. I'd stand more chance with her than his daughter.

Then I go outside and stroll around; just walking, knowing I can wake up tomorrow alive, that a shell won't scream down and blow me apart next moment.

I stop at a little *estaminet* and order a glass of wine; the thin red stuff you can drink all night. I'm wondering what to do next when I see someone looking at me from another table. Madam bloody Jessica. She picks up her drink, comes over and sits down without a 'by-your-leave'.

'Sure your doctor mates won't mind, Miss Collingwood? Associating with a common-as-cow-cakes sergeant.'

'I'll tell them you coerced me.' Still that same snooty way of speaking. 'They'll believe me and you'll probably be shot —'

'Muck off, you stupid bitch.'

She looks serious now, even embarrassed. I'm standing and she puts a gloved hand on my arm. 'Sorry, sergeant.' She sounds as though she means it. 'I heard about that poor soldier. It shouldn't have happened.'

'Well, a bloody doctor said Duncan was putting on an act.'

'To encourage the others,' she says bitterly. 'Can I buy you a drink?'

'I can buy my own.'

'Don't be a basket, Moran. I'm trying to apologise.'

'All right. Double cognac.'

So we sit and sip our drinks. She talks about the war, becoming a nurse. Her letters to Harry, returned when he was killed. 'I read them now and can't believe I'm the same person.' Then suddenly. 'How old are you?'

'Twenty.'

She looks at me. 'You enlisted when you were seventeen?'

'A lot of blokes did.'

'Harry did too. We both thought it was absolutely the right thing to do and it was — the way we thought then.'

She lights a cigarette and blows a smoke-ring; watches the night air pull it apart.

'Lost children,' she says.

I don't know what the hell that means. She blows another smoke-ring. 'I want this war to be over,' she says. 'Do you?'

'Sure.'

'Are you scared of the day it will end?'

I'm starting to get the pricker. That little hot angry feeling. What is all this stuff? Is she trying to show me how bloody clever she is?

Jessica orders coffee for us both; leans her elbows on the table and looks at me. 'The absence of war may destroy us.' I've had enough of this, but she goes on. 'What'll you do after the war, Moran? Go back to where you came from — with the thanks of a grateful Empire?'

I would go back to the slum street I came from. The booze, bread and dripping, bacon and tea. Shovelling coal or gravel in the railyards for ten bob a week. Maybe ending up like my dad.

'You're good at war, sergeant. You're good with men, a natural fighter. And you don't mind dying because life before this was hardly worth living.

Now you've got a uniform, a rifle — and enemies.'

The coffee comes. The waiter sloshes it into the saucer too, the way they do. She sips hers, looking moody. 'You're trained for war, to kill Germans. Do you think you'll be good at peace?'

'Dunno. Never thought about it.'

'I've got a responsible job and I save lives. For that matter, I'm not afraid of dying. Mother wrote the other day, remembered how nice I looked in pale pink chiffon.' For a moment I think she wanted to smash the coffee cup. 'I don't want to go back to chiffon and afternoon tea — ugh.'

'Then stay a nurse. I could stay a soldier. They owe us something.'

'You're a war-time soldier. I'm a war-time nurse. And yes, we're owed something, but do you think we'll get it? The establishment's like some bloody steam engine. It'll huff and puff, let off pressure — but grind us down because there's no room for us in peace, Jacko.'

'Jacko,' not 'sergeant.' She stands, not looking at me, and waits a moment, so I get up too, we walk off through the village, and get a strange look from two passing officers and sniggers from groups of drinking men — through the town till we're behind a row of little cottages, each with a pig snorting in the back garden.

Jessica's still talking. Like me, she's lost friends.

Nurses dead of typhus and pneumonia, even shellfire. One run over by a train. They get trench-foot too, as bad as ours. And work till they drop.

In the darkness she hugs me tight. It's like she needs reassurance. Then we sit on a low stone wall and she cries on my shoulder. It's not weakness, more like despair and anger — once she even beats her hand against my back.

'I don't want to think about home now,' she says once. 'It's somewhere unknown, somehow not real.'

Jessica pulls herself clear, blows her nose and lights another cigarette. I see her face in the flare of the match, closed and unhappy, and I realise my face is the same. I want this war to end, but peace frightens the hell out of me.

'If Harry could see me now,' she whispers at length.

'He wasn't the guy you said goodbye to. He'd understand.' He would. Our company was 98-strong in Gallipoli. Of all that first bunch, there's only me and Brasso left.

Her cigarette glows red in the darkness. She looks at me then we walk back through the narrow streets. They're still crowded with soldiers, will be most of the night. We pass stone knights in a row of alcoves in the big cathedral. The nurses' home is a big old stone convent behind it. Jessica takes my hand and pulls me firmly around to the side, by an outside staircase.

Her face is in darkness. 'My room's on the first floor.'

I don't say anything. I don't think she expects me to. She turns and walks up the stairs and they creak like hell. The creaking stops at the top with no sound of a door opening.

If a German soldier was in my sights, I would squeeze the trigger without delay, or stick my bayonet in a cornered rat. I'd pinch a bottle of wine without thinking twice or cheerfully boot a Scotsman right up his kilt. But I wait because, this time, I'm not sure of myself.

Then I think, what the hell? There's still fighting ahead, maybe another four years, maybe a Hun bullet with my name on it. So why think about the peace? Why think about any damned thing at all?

I go upstairs. Jessica is waiting at the top and opens the door.

PERHAPS GOING home should frighten me. Because going back up to the trenches is like 'home'. I am quiet, thinking about Jessica, and Brasso is sulking over his poker losses. Frog is bubbling about his two weeks; he spent them learning the history of the cathedral in the company of some old priest. He carries on about the stained-glass windows until Puha offers to chuck him through the next one we see.

I try writing to Jessica Collingwood twice, and both times I screw the letter up. She doesn't write to me.

We settle in. I prowl up and down our section, survey no-man's land with the trench periscopes. Brasso compares me to a dog sniffing out his new backyard.

We're good for each other, Brasso and me. I survive by getting out into no-man's land, forcing myself to think and live. He survives by dodging every damned thing except a fight. You have more chance of seeing the Kaiser using a spade than our Brasso.

We have our good-luck tokens too, though we don't call them that. Brasso's is his silver card-case with the Hun eagle on it. Mine is the Turk bullet with 'Faith' scratched on its brass case. We have these to keep us safe.

And I keep faith in myself by going out. It's a hunting tingle in me and I can't explain it any better. There is just me and the enemy. Rowlands doesn't want the Huns stirred up too much until his new boys have more experience, but he doesn't stop me going.

That black stink comes round me as I belly out, the sticky mud catching on my clothes. It seems there's always mud in no-man's land, even in the driest months. I have a hide just under a pile of black scrap iron. An aircraft engine — 'Sopwith Camel', of all funny names — that crashed and exploded. Burned bits of the dead pilot still crunch underfoot too.

My Mannlicher barrel scrapes on the rusted metal. Last time we were here, the Huns put up a sign. 'We have a coffin. Good kennel for the death-dog.' Oh sure, a joke in our trenches too, but like a good dog I didn't bite. Not with a dozen top marksmen hoping I would. But I didn't forget either and that's why I'm back.

There's an unusual noise as the sun comes up; a murmur of many voices, the stamp of many black-booted feet on the duckboards. There's a twinkling, flashing light as the dawn reflects off a bobbling line of periscopes. Even a chuckle or two.

I sight the Mannlicher and wait.

What's going on? There's a lot of Huns in there and they seem careless. Any moment now, one will want to be bolder than the others.

It comes with a head and shoulders outline, a peaked cap, not a spiked helmet, and he's using binoculars. Now voices are raised in sharp warning — too late.

Crack! The peaked cap flies up, bits of blood and brains with it. It falls upside down on the parapet, beside the binoculars, twilight flashing on the gold braid. The owner has fallen backward.

Something tells me to get the hell out, so I do. And next moment, pineapples rain down as the Hun mortars zero in. The machine-guns join in as I scramble and slosh through the shell-holes. Back in our trench, I get grumbles and black looks.

Everything was nice and quiet until Moran started the war again.

A FEW DAYS later we snatch two Hun soldiers. One is a tough little bugger out wire-slinging. He needs a rifle-butt on the head before we can drag him back to our trenches.

Back there, he comes to. Pig jerks a thumb at me — *Todeshund* — and he lashes out with his boot, jabbers something that sounds very rude.

Lieutenant Couch speaks some German and explains. The Hun I sniped was a 'Graf', their name for an Earl. Related to the Hun Royal Family and a personal mate of the Kaiser's. Easily (says Couch, keeping his face straight) the most important person I've killed.

Brasso says cheerfully he's not taking money on me coming back any more. That my goose is cooked if the Huns get hold of me now. They don't like snipers at the best of times — but the Kaiser's own mate?

Rowlands is concerned too, not for my skin though. The Graf commanded a Bavarian division, last heard of on the Eastern Front. So what were he and his staff doing in the front trenches? And our lines falling quiet again, as though the Huns didn't want to start anything — yet.

The Hun wire-slinger won't tell us anything, but we have more luck with his mate. He's seventeen, a fat little mamma's boy who I nicknamed Rupert. The name *Todeshund* just about makes him pee. He talks so much we can't stop him.

Lieutenant Couch translates. Yes, a big party of top officers went into the forward trenches. Graf Wilhelm boasted he was not afraid of Tommy bullets — and got one. And yes, troop-trains from the Eastern Front were coming in all the time. Artillery, more than he had ever seen. I scowl at him and he blubbers about '*Flammenwerfer*' and '*Sturmtruppen*.'

'Flamethrowers and stormtroopers,' interprets Couch quietly.

Just then the real Rupert (Major Creel) comes up. Creel in the front trenches is like cream-buns for lunch — never happens. He shakes his head, the smug shit — more troops and artillery? Of course, for defence, there's half a million Yanks coming.

And the Germans, says Creel, smirking all over his pink face, cannot match that number. And *why* (this was Couch's slip) is this snivelling ninny referred to as Rupert?

'Ruprecht,' says Couch quickly, 'named after the Crown Prince.'

Creel takes the prisoners down to headquarters.

Up and down the line, other prisoners are brought in and say the same thing. That more troops and guns are moving up to our Front. And the staff react like Creel — it's all defence, the Germans don't have another punch left in them.

Yes, and they're beaten, half-starved. Their allies, Turkey and Austria, are collapsing — that's why they've pulled back to the Hindenburg Line — to hold here and wait for peace-terms.

Every soldier in the front line knows this is crap. The Huns are fighters and there's lots of fight left in them. We can smell what's coming — like a hunting-dog smelling the wild pig. We know they are coming.

A Hun patrol chucks a dog's skull into our lines. On the skull, a red-lettered word. *Todeshund*. I don't need a translator for that message.

WE PULL BACK to the second line. The same rumours when we go up to the Front again. More build-ups and more troops. And our generals, of course, say the Huns are on their last legs.

I go out into no-man's land again. Not without another 'Pitcher and Well' lecture from Rowlands. Yeah, screw you, Mr Rowlands. I take the dog-skull with me. I wait for a Hun patrol on their way back — they see the dog-skull. They stop a moment, all I need.

Two of them dead and I get no more messages.

The Front stays quiet but more deserters come

in. The same story, more artillery and troops. All those divisions pulled back from Russia and coming our way.

The staff say not to worry.

Dog skull

'I HAVEN'T SEEN Ellen or Kate, think Kate's got a kid now. You heard about Dad — yeah. I don't mind the army. Good grub and clothes. They even fixed my teeth.' Georgie calls me Bob. I'm so used to Jacko that Bob sounds strange now. He's looking at me too, like I'm someone he doesn't know. 'You're different,' he says. 'Look a hell of a lot older.'

'You try a couple of years in the trenches.'

He's taller than I remember. Hair cut short, the freckles gone. His equipment is clean; he'll make a good soldier. We're in an *estaminet* just outside Amiens. Rowlands gave me a twenty-four hour pass to see him.

At least our blokes are trained well. His battalion's in a holding camp nearby, and go up the line tomorrow.

He listens to me, to my hints on how to stay alive. He grimaces at the thought of lice or rats. 'Sounds like home,' he jokes. Sure, but we didn't have rotting corpses for neighbours.

We eat bread, sausage and the gooey white cheese, and drink the thin red wine. Georgie loves all this, it's different and exciting. And he's heard about Jacko the deadly sniper. My duel with Dead Willi made the home papers and Dad got free drinks for a week.

It's good to see him. He looks up to me, so life means a bit more than it did. The Moran brothers. It sounds good; he even wonders I know a few words in French. I tell him not to be a sniper.

When the truck I'm getting a ride back on comes, we shake hands and I wave to him from the back. He stays by the roadside till we're out of sight.

I hope he comes through. If he remembers everything I told him, he's got a chance. On the way back, I'm thinking. I've stacked up some goodwill with Rowlands; maybe I can work a transfer. Bypass Creel and go straight to Colonel Fields.

That night I tell Rowlands and he nods.

Next day he tells me to go to headquarters — has he worked it that quickly? HQ is a big reinforced dugout about a mile behind the firing line, with telephone wire strung everywhere.

Fields was our company captain at Gallipoli. He's a colonel now, and changed like us all; only forty, but grey hair. His hands shake a little bit and his eyes are red-rimmed. I tell him why I've come and he pours me a drink!

'Get that down you.'

I do so and, even as I swallow, realise something is wrong. *Oh God, don't let it be that!*

He's already speaking, shuffling papers as he does. He's just heard the news and was about to call Rowlands. The Germans laid down a box barrage on the new troop-draft at a crossroads. The result was sixty per cent casualties. Private George Moran was one.

I just looked at him. I don't salute, just get up and go. A ration carrier gets in my way up the communication trench and I shove him aside. There's something bitter and confused inside me — different emotions punching each other hard — like I was being punched too.

No more Moran Brothers. Kate and Ellen might not know unless they read the casualty lists. I doubt that they do.

Back in the trenches that night, it hits me. I have nothing now but my uniform stripes, my Mannlicher, this trenchline and a few mates. And that only until the war ends.

Jessica Collingwood is right. The end of the war means nothing to people like us.

No-man's land and a little firestorm breaks out. It's been quiet, then some fool fires at the wrong time and another fool joins in. Then the machine-guns start and suddenly the air is full of sleeting lead like rain.

I went on a little one-man recce patrol last night, checking on a new Hun observation post. We'll raid it, bomb it, maybe grab another prisoner and hear more about the big offensive that staff don't think will happen.

So it's dawn, lighter than I like it. I'm edging back from shell-crater to shell-crater and a flare bursts overhead. I'm muddy, flat to the ground and the firing starts. I take a header into the next shell-hole and somebody is already there, long grey overcoat, spiked helmet. I'm unslinging my rifle as he turns.

I have the rifle out, he has a Luger. One of those long-barrelled nine-shot jobs. His eyes glitter under his helmet. We both pause that moment — *why!* But we do and it's a stand-off. If I press the trigger, so will he. Even if I killed him, his dead finger would twitch on the trigger and not miss.

The bullet-storm is dying away, quick as it began. We look at each other. He's thickset, older than me, a big fair moustache like those photos of the Kaiser. The Luger is rock-steady.

He shouts something in German.

I shake my head. 'Don't speak Hun.'

The last shots are fired, a final long burst of machine-gun fire. He speaks again, his eyes intent. No, you won't fox me like that, waiting for a careless moment to press the trigger. I keep my eyes and my gun on him. He points down with his free hand.

You don't get me like that, either! I've already seen the dead man, probably killed last night. Right, so you were looking for him.

'Brudder,' he says, or something like it.

All right mate, lots of brothers dead — *yeah, Georgie!*

Now his eyes widen because he's seen my rifle and telescopic sights. *'Ach … Mannlicher … der Todeshund … Teufel!'*

I don't know what that last word means. Something rude, the Huns don't like me.

It's much lighter now and staying here will kill us both. The German knows that too. He extends his hand, encased in a thick leather gauntlet, points to his side of the lines, points at me and jerks a thumb to my side.

Easy enough to understand. Let's go our separate ways.

It's a good idea. I am sweating already and I don't want to blink it out of my eyes, those Lugers have hair triggers.

So I nod and he inches carefully sideways. I do the same. I note the collar tabs on his overcoat — he's a captain — *Hauptmann* they call them. As he moves, he reaches down and very slowly, takes a brown leather wallet from the dead man, with a gold watch looped around it. Letters or photos? Or maybe he is just trying to distract me.

I'm sweating now and so is he. My breath dry and loud. A fly buzzes loudly, settles on my forehead. *Leave it there!* We move carefully, slowly. Now he stops, then inches up the side of the shell-crater.

How the hell does he scramble over? Or me? Both at the same time? Then who gives the signal? We don't even understand each other. He seems to know this, slaps his holster with his free hand and points to the top. Then a pushing motion — put your rifle up. I nod.

We are inching to the top. I don't know what goes wrong. Maybe his coat-sleeve catches in something. But his gun-hand jerks, I fling sideways as he fires and my bullet hits his gun, knocking it from his hand.

I work the bolt and see him flinch. He's dead and knows it. His mouth tightens his hand clutching the leather wallet. Now I can blink and quickly wipe my forehead.

The younger man looks asleep. A smaller version of the same moustache, looks like him. So he came here for his brother's personal effects — *that doesn't mean I spare you!* His mouth goes tighter, he growls something, that sounds like 'Get on with it.'

'Piss off, you stupid sausage-eating mucker.'

He doesn't understand but his eyes widen when

I point to the Hun trenchline. He's still thinking I'll kill him, but I won't. I'm thinking about me going back for Georgie — *you'll never know Georgie saved your life.* Georgie dead, I should shoot him just for that — *so why the hell not?*

'Move!' What do they yell to their men when attacking? *'Raus!'*

So he scrambles over the edge, flinching at the top, expecting a bullet. The younger man lies there, dead, but no sign of a mark. I could've taken that captain back. He wouldn't have spared me. I will have to watch that. Being merciful.

It might get me killed.

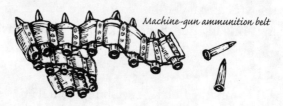

Machine-gun ammunition belt

WE ARE IN the second trenchline again and the Staff want an urgent report; probably something important like how many broken boot-laces we've got. Major Creel is nowhere around so Captain Rowlands asks Sergeant Moran if he wants to see how the other half lives. His words, not mine.

So it's full uniform, boots polished, medals displayed, whistles and jeers from the lads as I take off in the sidecar of a despatch rider.

The noise of war fades to a dull mutter as we drive for nearly half an hour. Finally, we're on a long road untouched by shellfire and lined with trees. There's a huge white stone that says this one was built by a Lord de la Somebody about five hundred years ago.

IT'S LIKE another world. A smartly-uniformed groom goes past with two glossy black horses because the Staff like their morning rides. There's an officer, in tunic, bright boots and riding breeches, who ignores me.

In the main hall, the duty sergeant, red-faced and nearly bursting out of his bright-buttoned tunic, speaks like a dog barking. His eyes pop a little at seeing my Cross. He sends an orderly with me. Everyone has spotless white gloves on.

There's a lot of officers out back, welcoming yet another group of fact-finding politicians. To stop them finding out too much, says the orderly with a grin. There's a big striped awning because the sun's a bit hot, and I remember those wounded soldiers lying in the rain.

A band is playing soft music. A long table laden with bottles and food, served by waiters in white coats. Ham, chicken, strawberries and cream in big pitchers. I've forgotten about food like that.

The officer I want comes over from the top-hatted politicians in long black coats. He notes my

Cross, takes the report and nods. Red-faced and purple-nosed, white whiskers and bristling eyebrows; a jolly face and not-so-jolly grey eyes. I've met jolly-faced bastards like him before.

'So you're Moran, the deadly En-Zed sniper?' his words loud so the politicians can hear. 'Potted lots of Huns lately? Had something to eat?' He clicks his fingers and a waiter brings little triangular sandwiches on a silver tray. 'Help yourself,' he booms. 'Take a handful.'

This is for the politicians, not me. They nod approvingly at this nice display for comrades-in-arms. His pale grey eyes glint like burning flares — be careful, you bloody nobody non-com.

'Thank you, sir,' I say, the little too-cheeky smile that officers know. *Sod you, whiskers!*

'Dismissed, sergeant.' He gets the message, those pale eyes glint. 'Wouldn't mind having a crack myself. Dashed good fun — what?'

We go back through the chateau — oak-panelled walls, thick carpet in the big rooms and long oil paintings. The place stinks of rank and luxury and you can't even hear the war.

I can still hear the band playing as we drive off. I bite one of the sandwiches and spit it out. Cucumber or something. The wind blasts my face and I pull my cap low.

I'm thinking on the way home. Daydreaming

rather. One Hun shell would wipe out all of them but their guns don't reach this far. I could have potted a few with my Mannlicher though, before the others scattered.

By Jove, that'd be dashed good fun — what?

It's February, and still quiet. The Hun aircraft are machine-gunning our trenches and dropping small bombs, working each sector in turn. This week it's our turn.

The Hun pilots are very good. They come in low and should be sitting ducks but they're not. Hitting an aircraft from the ground is damned hard. They fly through everything we can chuck at them and down come those nasty little bombs. One takes out an Ob. post and two men. A shark-like Albatross, turning to come back. The aircraft is striped black and yellow like a wasp. I elbow Frog off the Vickers and remember the gunnery tips that young pilot taught me. I shout to the men to fire in front, so the plane flies into the bullets.

It comes in so low, I can see the goggled head of the pilot. His twin guns streak black bullet-lines at me. The Vickers jars in my hands — *it's working* — bullets hit the engine and the propeller flies to pieces.

He's going too fast to pull out. He hits no-man's land, his wings tear off, like ripped from a bird, with a horrible great splintering crash. An explosion and fire.

I push Frog back on the Vickers. Everyone cheers and even Creel comes up to tell Frog that was worth a bottle of rum. What a face-change when he learns who did it.

'Never mind the rum, sir,' I say. 'Gets in the way sometimes.'

He knows exactly what I mean. His breath stinks of it. He gives me a look and stalks off. No matter, the rat hates me anyway.

Out in no-man's land, the crashed aircraft burns into the night.

Vickers gun

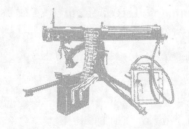

March 21, 1918. 4.18 a.m.

'WE'VE GOT about twenty minutes,' murmurs Rowlands. 'The Hun is usually punctual on such occasions.'

It's a quiet cold, dark morning and the metal of our guns is like ice. Our trenchline and firing-step are fully manned for this stand-to, ordered because we believe the Huns are finally about to attack. At 4.40 a.m.

It's now 4.15 a.m. and bloody cold. There's white mist forming in no-man's land and it's drizzling, wet — it always seems to be wet before a Hun offensive. Maybe they really can control the weather, as Pig's always saying. Out in that misty darkness it is very quiet.

Well, *are* they finally coming? Deserters are saying so, but they will say anything. We were on stand-to last night and the night before, four nights last week. I look at my watch again. 4.20.

'They're not making any noise about it, sir,' I mutter to Rowlands. 'Hasn't even been wire-cutting patrols out.'

'They don't need them,' he mutters back. 'They've got new proximity fuses on their shells, which explode if they touch a hair, let alone wire.'

Creel is up amongst us, ordered by Colonel Fields I think, who is wise to him. He is huddled in long coat and cap with his hands in his pockets, shivering — with cold, I suppose.

'I hope they come,' whispers Rowlands, his lips almost brushing the frost-rimed sandbags on the parapet. 'This war must end, it must.'

That reminds me of something else Pig says. The war will end when the last soldier is dead.

'Do you know what's so bloody silly about this?' Is Rowlands talking to me or himself? 'If Britain and France lose the war, they'll only lose colonies, and maybe some of their Navy. The Kaiser and our Royal Family are related. He's not going to overturn the power of kings, not after what happened in Russia.'

His breath comes out in frosty steam. 'Thank about that, Moran. We'll go home and it will all be the same. The Huns don't give a toss about New Zealand or Australia. Or Canada.'

'Sir?'

Never has Rowlands talked like this. Maybe Creel has overheard because he comes over, booted feet jarring the duckboards.

No, for another reason, more typically Creel. 'Another false alarm, Rowlands. Looks like Jerry isn't coming. Think I'll —'

'It's only 4.30, sir,' interrupts Rowlands and he's never done that before either. 'The Jerry said 4.40, remember?'

I enjoy the look on Creel's face. 'Maybe the

Germans are just making sure we lose our beauty sleep, sir,' I say in a low voice with a cheerful smile.

'Shut up, sergeant.' He stamps off. Rowlands shrugs. Ahead now, the white mist is a little thicker.

'Maybe the Germans *can* control the weather,' I mutter to Rowlands.

'Only God can do that, to the best of my knowledge, sergeant,' he says. 'And God knows whose side He is on.'

4.33 a.m.

There is not a damn sound out there, not even the little noises of rats among the dead, as though they sense something too. Or is all this just getting on my nerves? Of course there won't be a noise. The artillery will open first — all those field-guns from the Eastern Front, each with huge stacks of shells that our spotter aircraft have seen. They've got enough for a week's constant firing, just to soften us up.

If it *is* about to start.

I mention this to Rowlands. 'Should be all right, sir. Our reserves must be coming up.'

'No.' Rowlands is speaking very quietly now, but like he wants to get it off his chest. 'HQ says Fifth Army Command asked for them but was refused. Staff thinks the French'll be clobbered, not us.'

'*Shit!* You mean —'

'I mean, sergeant, I hope very much this is a false alarm.'

4.37 a.m.

If Rowlands is wrong, we have three minutes to go.

My Enfield is resting on the sandbagged parapet, a stack of magazine clips ready for 'Mad Minute' shooting. Rowlands looks almost dreamy as he traces a gloved finger down the rifle-stock, leaving a long wet streak.

'They only had muzzle-loading flintlocks at Waterloo, sergeant. "Brown Bess", they nicknamed it. Know your Kipling?'

No, Mr Soddin' Rowlands, it's 4.39 and I don't know what sodding Waterloo was or Kipling from a bloody red herring. He's quoting very softly.

'And everyone bowed as she opened the ball … on the arm of a high-gaitered grim grenadier.'

4.40.

It's going to start now, if it starts. Mr Rowlands knows this, the whole trench does. Utter silence, like everyone is holding their breath. Rowlands pauses for a moment then goes on talking.

' "Brown Bess." Should the Enfield have a nick-name? Odd how we personalise them, always as the gentler sex. Any idea why, sergeant?'

4.42.

'No, sir.'

There's murmuring along the trench now and some idiot lights up. I stop that with a savage whisper.

Creel splashes up again in his nice leather boots. Brisk now — thinking about bacon and eggs and coffee, back in the second line. 'As I thought, Rowlands, another no-show. If anyone wants me —'

4.43.

I should be used to it — I always think I am. But that first moment — when it's like the world exploding — catches me like a dog catching a rabbit. The first shells scream over, like devils are riding them, and the world really does explode.

Two thousand guns have opened up all along the line and down comes the hell-shower of high explosive, phosgene, mustard gas, even the dreaded white phosphorus.

'Gas masks!' yells Rowlands.

Yellow gas clouds are forming among the high explosive. I fumble for the tin container, pull the mask out. The eyeholes already misted, better to be blind than cough my lungs to mince-meat. Pounding and crashing of shells, the shock-waves punch me like a fist.

Already men are falling, sandbags flung up into the air. Duckboards splintered, slapping sideways. Creel is yelling, unheard in the din, then a shell-blast throws him flat — *I forgive the Huns anything to see that!*

Shellfire punches, whacks, deafens. It goes on and on like hammers exploding, concussing us. And the gas clouds drift in, thick and greasy; the phone wires cut, but this din is up and down the lines. The white mist is coloured a muddy yellow now. Our gunners have joined in but they are lost in the great Hun barrage.

Creel staggers into his dug-out, only stunned — *damn and blast!* The cut phone-lines gave him the usual excuse to scramble back to the second trenches. One shell explodes right inside the trench — screams, eight men killed, a leg flies into the air.

Now the trench is a butcher's mess, a bloody shambles. More shells right on us as the Hun gunners find our range. Bodies torn, gutted, intestines strung like red sausages over the torn sandbags. I am running down the trench, being knocked over, knocked sideways, yelling for the men to take over. No cover though, from the crashing pounding devil's noise that goes on and on. Like we are trapped inside a huge pounding drum.

In no-man's land, the mist and gas-smoke are plucked aside, the wire is beaten down. Our faces raw from the gas-masks, our machine-gunners take off goggles to peer through the mist, leaving nose clip and mouth-piece in place. Frog's eyes are streaming with tears, not crying — it's the new 'tear-gas'.

And this should only be the beginning. It should go on for some days because then, even our High Command would get reserves up. Days, even weeks, but five hours later it suddenly stops and out of the mist and smoke come the German storm-troopers and among them, men with big metal canisters on their backs and pipes that hose flame.

Flammenwerfer!

So suddenly, so quick. No time to call our artillery, even if the lines were not cut. Frog's Vickers starts, I shout for men to man the trenches but they are slow, dulled by that awful hell. Brasso has the other Vickers, now we are manning the parapet and the rattle of small-arms fire replaces the thunder.

We can't stop them!

This time the Germans keep coming. They were already halfway across when we spotted them, when the barrage rose. They are in A company's trenches and storming along, clearing saps and dugouts with bombs and flamethrowers.

Norris yells, drops his rifle and jumps back from the firing step. I make to grab him and am knocked aside by A Company men running down our trench-line. Now more men are dropping off the firing step. Rowland and Couch shout at them, revolvers in hand, but they are running — *running!*

'Pull back!' Rowlands shouts to me. 'Have to regroup!'

Regroup where? Our second-line trenches are being pounded too and there are no reserves for a counter-attack. I tell Frog to take the Vickers, Pig helps him, trailing belts of ammo. We can see spiked helmets and grey uniforms at the other end of the trench now — and on the parapet.

I push the last soldier onto the communication trench, Mannlicher over my shoulder, Enfield in hand. A bullet smashes it away, I sling the Mannlicher around, sunlight flashing on the telescopic sights. Shouts of anger; they all know that gun.

'*Todeshund — der Todeshund!*'

German soldiers drop into our trenches, the duckboards flopping. Raising their rifles to fire. Then a loud yammering in my ear and two Huns are flung back. Brasso with the light Lewis, now clicking on empty. He shouts, throwing a grenade.

'Come on, you mucking no-hoper!'

An explosion, the first Huns flung aside. Grenade bits have hit a *flammenwerfer* — what a sight! Swinging around in his death-agony, the Huns ducking their own arcing spray of fire. A bright ball of flame from his tank — he explodes!

Brasso pulls me back down the trench and we stumble over a dead body — Norris. I want to thank Brasso but he slaps me. 'Not getting off that easy, you still owe me a quid from blackjack!'

Now the German shells are falling around us with good coordination, pushing us out of the second line, their stormtroopers coming on in the teeth of it, and we are back at the reserve line. *We've never pushed so far*. And they keep coming, well-trained soldiers, taking losses but always attacking.

We are pushed back further, we cannot stand. Our flanks are battered in. This is not just a reverse to be rallied by a counter attack. Now our troops are stumbling across fields where the only shell-craters are new; created by the Hun artillery. This is retreat.

Rowlands, bandaged, his coat torn across, keeps us together. Creel is nowhere to be seen. Half of us are dead, wounded or missing. In the morning light there are patches of misty yellow gas. The roads are choked with horses, guns, wagons and shuffling crowds of men, ignoring their officers.

Behind comes the boom-crump, boom-crump of Hun artillery and through their own gas-clouds, masked lines of Hun soldiers, seeming endless.

Retreat.

IT'S LIKE AN almighty kick in the guts. Our generals always said the trenchline would be broken; after four years of war, it has finally happened … but not by us. By the Germans with one single massive punch.

They did it by not waiting for the Americans. They did everything our generals said they wouldn't do. They used seventy divisions, a hundred and forty thousand men, to tear a hole right through the Fifth Army.

In the first day alone, they advance twenty miles.

At the end of that day, thirty thousand British and Allied troops are dead, wounded, or prisoner.

On that first day they won ground that cost us four years of blood.

And the retreat goes on.

Spandau machine-gun

ON THE SECOND day we try and rally at a ridge and row of trees. German aircraft fly overhead and drop flares; next moment the Hun artillery shells are dropping around us. On our left, a rag-tag of British conscripts give way. Their officer shoots one, the others just keep running.

The Hun soldiers come on in line, 'like beaters flushing game,' yells Couch bitterly, waving their helmets. More shells howl towards us like devil's laughter.

Another ridge, then a shattered village, but it's the same; the shells scream down, the Hun soldiers attack, flushed with victory. Ours are shocked, leaderless and stunned; they will not stand.

We hear the Huns have taken Albert. They are pressing on to Bapaume. Rowlands mutters that they are driving a wedge between the British and French armies. If they do, then the French will fall back on Paris; the British on the Channel Ports.

And that will be the end. The Germans will win the war.

We fall back.

'SEE THIS,' says Rowlands.

Sometimes we turn when the Huns get too bold. This time, catching their advance in a bloody little ambush. Some two hundred, caught in our crossfire; Rowlands is kneeling by one, pointing to a stripe on the cuff of his sleeve.

'Battle honour,' he says, 'from about a hundred and fifty years ago. Saxon regiment; they were British allies then, helped us win our battles.'

'Who were we fighting then?'

'France, I believe.'

The French. Our allies now. Rowlands gets up, unsteadily shoves his revolver into the holster. His voice cracked dry, I hand him my canteen. He's nearly dead on his feet, his face smudged thickly with dirt, unshaven; we all look the same.

'Next one might be for beating England and France — makes sense, sarge?'

Rum and water in my canteen, he swallows loudly. The bitter note in his voice stops, like he's choked it back.

Like we're all choking back one thought; the Huns are pushing us hard, already their artillery are dropping shells. We yell orders, the men get into order.

Brasso loots a last body — the Saxon with the battle-stripe on his sleeve.

We fall back, fall back, go on falling back.

We pass two elderly nuns sitting in those green canvas chairs the artillery use. Rowlands tries out his French on them, the Huns are coming and artillery shells do not respect civilians. They understand but shake their heads.

We see a line of wounded French soldiers, too badly hurt to travel. Most are dying. The nuns are staying because of them. We look away and keep going.

Further down we find a single British field-gun with a wounded officer and two gunners. They've had no orders to retire, he says, and will engage the Huns over open sights. A year ago — a week ago — we might have stayed to help but not now.

Rowlands throws him a salute. Later, we hear the crump-boom of a single gun. It only goes on a few minutes, replaced by distant rifle-fire.

We are part of a jostling mob now and most have thrown away their weapons. In two days the Huns are fifty miles deep inside our lines.

Shoving us back, back.

SOME TIME in that week we lose touch with our rear guard and Rowlands sends me, Brasso and Pig to find them. We commandeer a truck packed with officers' luggage. Brasso backhands the driver away, and Pig and I kick out the suitcases as he drives us back. Freshly-laundered shirts and underwear scatter after us, a crate of expensive champagne smashes and Pig howls with dismay.

Brasso stops at a peach orchard. We can hear firing. We go through the trees, ripe fruit squashing underfoot. There's a stores depot ahead. Now the Germans have it.

The troops are out of control, looting. Their officers wave swords and shoot in the air but it's no use. Some soldiers are drinking, but most are cramming food into their mouths. Others are staggering under armloads of food and cigarettes.

'Army rations,' whispers Brasso, 'if that doesn't kill them, nothing will.'

A soldier staggers near us with an armload of cans and flops down, singing drunkenly. He opens the cans with his bayonet and empties them into his helmet. Bully beef. He puts it on, chuckling as the mess is squeezed out over his face, licking it off.

An officer runs up and whacks him with the flat of his sword. The soldier just rolls over and goes to sleep.

Our food depots delay the Hun more than we do. They are half-starved, the soldiers always stopping to plunder and eat and drink.

There's no sign of our men and we go back. Brasso steers the truck over those nice clean shirts and underwear; tangling them into the mud. The truck runs out of petrol and we abandon it.

No end in sight.

Sometimes we stop and fight. More rag-tag groups, British, Aussies, French and us. The Hun advance slows as the generals frantically throw in more troops. Units from anywhere, even cooks and drivers; untrained conscripts straight from England. They die or they run.

WE CROSS A river. Our engineers fail to blow the bridge and the Germans follow. A cursing, white-faced, French major with a broken sword rallies us. '*Mes braves, mes braves,*' he shouts hoarsely and leads a counter-attack. It is shot to pieces, along with the major.

We are pushed back to another broken village. Hun aircraft come and the flares drop. Shellfire explodes around us, one in the ruins of a brick cottage. Beside me, a sound I will never forget as Brasso screams.

His face took the full force of the blast; fragments of brickwork smashing into him. Now it's a tattered bloody mask, he's still screaming. There's no drugs, I have to smack him under the jaw to silence him. I wrap a field-dressing around his head.

A last truck is going, I stop it. The driver protests

that he hasn't got room, then finds himself looking at Rowlands' revolver. So he finds room for Brasso in the back. Brasso is moaning, his bandages already bloody, but he's got a chance.

The Huns behind, like a bloody great shunting engine, coming on, coming on, coming on.

WE TRY TO regroup by another orchard. Peach trees again and apples. Rowlands says this area is famous for its cider. The farmer, his wife and two little girls are out among the trees. There is always work to do, even though the guns are thundering away.

Maybe generations of his family will have worked on those trees, says Trent, a fruitgrower. They are busy and do not stop to wave. They have seen soldiers pass many times.

Another attack and more lives wasted. The Germans are just too strong. Later that same day, we retreat past the same orchard.

In the meantime, the Germans have shelled the road and anything that could be used as a strongpoint. Now the trees are shattered, stripped of bark and branches; the way shell fragments will strip man of his skin. They are all broken and dead. No shell-craters, must have been shrapnel. Maybe the Germans thought troops were hiding there.

The farmer and one daughter are lying dead among their trees. The wife must have caught up the other girl; they nearly made it to the house before the shells got them. They are lying across the open doorway.

We don't stop. We have no plans to use this place as a strongpoint. Black crows flutter among the broken trees as we pass on. Sleep-walking, bone tired, moving back like it's bloody habit now.

WE'RE IN THE woods near Bapaume just before it falls. The Huns on our heels, moving bloody fast, field-guns towed behind horses and trucks.

We keep a sharp lookout for their aircraft as we enter the woods. If we're spotted, the shells are soon falling, bang-crump, bang-crump — or if they're gas-shells, whiz-plop, whiz-plop. We're so busy watching the sky that we nearly trip over what's ahead.

A British battalion in full battle-order. The sharpshooters out front, rifle-butts pressed to their cheeks. Then lines of soldiers, rifle in one hand, grenade in the other. Machine-gunners in the after-noon sunlight, goggling like they're all wearing monkey-masks.

They are dead, every man-jack of them.

They were spotted and the gas-shells were plop-ping among them as they frantically put on their gas-masks. They got them on and died anyway. One officer was lying there, binoculars still to his eyes. We took rifles and ammunition. Even the machine-guns, but nobody tries to force grenades from those dead hands.

The sweetish sticky trace of gas is still in the air. We keep moving, out of those silent trees, away from the bodies of six hundred men.

The retreat goes on.

IT GOES ON, always the same. Sometimes we counter-attack to slow down the Hun advance. But always they have more men and more guns — and the drive of troops who know they are winning. We are bone-tired, staggering from lack of sleep. The days are more like weeks on these muddy roads. Somewhere we will have to turn and fight. Otherwise this will be the end.

I catch myself wondering if I care. Whoever owns Europe means nothing to me. But I'm a soldier in my third year of war and fighting is my job, so I do it. The only job I'm good at.

I come awake one morning after two hours' sleep. Breakfast is half an army biscuit and rainwater from a puddle. Rowlands is as unshaven and filthy as the rest of us, nearly dead on his feet. He nudges me, his voice hoarse as he points ahead.

'See that!'

'That' is something like a tiny needle in the distance. It means nothing to me. 'The spire of Amiens Cathedral,' he gasps, gulping rainwater. It trickles over the thick stubble on his chin. 'If we can't stop the Huns at Amiens … then we can't stop them.'

The Germans have been pressing us hard since they took the bridges. They want Amiens. But all this ground is broken from the old Somme battlefields; craters and trench work grassed over now, slowing us down, and the Huns — white bones sticking out of the ground. And later that day I see something I will never forget.

There's a drumming sound behind us and Rowlands turns. So does Pig, his mouth gaping. I am helping Frog clear a jam in the Vickers; the little beggar has carried it all this way, one lens of his spectacles broken and a dirty bandage around his head. Then he looks over behind us.

'Oh cripes almighty,' he breathes.

Which is very strong language for Frog so I turn. There's some clear ground around us, and cresting a rise comes a line of lance-points. Then helmeted heads and horse's heads. Cavalry, line after line of them in perfect order. One of those regiments who've spent the war waiting for our breakthrough, which never came.

They sweep down in perfect order at the canter. Officers ahead, with drawn swords flashing. Down come the lance points and tiny flags flutter in the breeze. A bugle blast and the canter becomes a charge.

The first German troops are less than a mile away, only forward units, and they stand still, taken by surprise. Then, over the drumming hoofbeats comes a German bugle. The line of men spreads out, they lie flat. A machine-gun is hastily fitted to its tripod, just a thin skirmish line against that thundering mass of horsemen. It looks too bloody thin.

Then the firing starts. The flat 'Toc, toc' of the Mauser rifles, the stutter of a machine-gun, gunsmoke and the crump-boom of a field-gun in action.

The lancers go down. It is the bravest thing I have ever seen and the worst massacre. Men and horses, rolling over and over like shot rabbits. The first line, then the second line. Some lancers scramble up and run alongside the mounted, a hand on the stirrup; the bullets get them and they go down.

We are helpless to do anything but watch. Only a handful get to the German skirmish line. One officer, waving his sword, he's pulled from his horse and bayoneted. A German soldier lies skewered with a lance. But the fight is brief because most of the lancers lie on the field in their rows and clumps of dead.

The firing stops, replaced by the screams of mangled and dying horses.

'Lancers,' says Rowlands quietly. 'Death or glory boys.'

They could have got away with that charge,

about five hundred years ago, before guns were invented, and charges like that did slow the Germans a little bit even now. So we take up position outside Amiens, with the town and cathedral spire five miles behind.

Somehow we sort ourselves out. A ratbag army of French, Scots, Canadians, Aussies, English and us. We dig in, arm as best we can and wait. The Channel Ports are behind Amiens.

No more retreat. Here we must stand or die.

Mannlicher

THE GERMANS have taken twelve hundred square miles of ground and they're forty miles deep in our broken lines. They have taken nearly a thousand guns and nearly a hundred thousand prisoners.

Another hundred thousand are dead or wounded.

Before Amiens, we form a fighting line of forti-fied points around shell-craters and connecting trenches. We are more or less re-formed and some reinforcements arrive. There are a lot of men missing, but Creel is not one of them. We have to fight because we are too tired to run.

So we dig in and wait. The Hun is coming, but

he gives us a day or so. His own troops are just as tired and hungrier than us, stopping to loot our depot. But they are coming.

Overhead, their fighters and ours criss-cross in air battles. Their top pilot, that 'Red Baron' is shot down. But here, in the mud and shell-holes, is where it will be decided.

'Can't find out what happened to Brasso,' says Rowlands. 'He could be anywhere, we won't know till things settle down.'

'So things are going to settle down, sir?'

Rowlands laughs. 'Better ask the Hun High Command or even the Kaiser. He's given all the German kids a day off school in celebration of victory.'

'I left school early, sir.'

We are in the main fortified post. Most of it is a big shell-crater, maybe made by a 155mm gun. The Germans have a monster cannon now, shelling Paris from seventy miles away. Our post is lined with sand-bags, duckboards. Frog and Pig are setting up the Vickers and digging a little bay for the ammunition.

Our own High Command has told us to hold at all costs. Divisions are coming up — they say. And our battalion will be reinforced by a Highland one soon. Even Creel is ordered to stay in the front line.

Rowlands is eating from a tin of bully beef with the tip of a bayonet. He passes the tin to me and I use my fingers.

'Flanders, 1916, sergeant. Just you and me out of that first bunch.'

'And Pig, sir.'

Rowlands chuckles. 'I was forgetting Pig.' He gives a weary sigh. 'I'll be glad when this is over.'

'Over, sir?'

Rowlands rubs a hand over his face. He spent last night writing to his wife and I've never seen him so tired. 'One way or another, sergeant, it will be over. We'll be in Berlin or the Kaiser will be in London. Then … peace.'

Which, after three years of war, means nothing to me.

It's still only the end of March. We've got another 5 a.m. start to battle when the Germans come.

Their first attack is like a wave, a long way out to sea. It comes in slowly but gathers speed as it nears the land. It gets bigger and bigger, until suddenly it's too big and crashes over you.

Their guns bombard us, their aircraft swoop with those bloody flares. Then comes the infantry. I never knew how many of those seventy divisions were left — I thought we'd cut down a good few of them. But there are still too many and we begin blasting away.

Stormtroopers and flame-throwers front their attack. But in the face of our fire, none of them get close enough. I spin one around with a lucky shot, he burns like a torch. I think of Brasso saving me, hope to God he's still alive.

The Germans keep coming. There are old shell-craters, even the sunken lines of old trenches from 1916 when this was a battleground. They can take cover and be reinforced while we lose men.

Beside me, a man is flung back — bullet between the eyes. Another just slumps quietly down as though resting. A third screams as a bullet smashes his shoulder. Frog and Pig are firing the Vickers, Rowlands yelling for us to hold — hold!

The rifle thumps my shoulder as I fire. My ears are deafened by noise, my face crusted with mud. *This is battle, where I belong!* So let them come. If this is my last fight, the Huns will know they fought *Todeshund*.

THROUGH THE day we hold them. There are break-throughs, posts overrun. We counter-attack, meet the Germans in no-man's land with bayonets, fists and knives, slipping in the muck.

At evening the close fighting stops but the Huns don't withdraw. Artillery takes over, the sky goes blue-black; the flares climb and burst into red, yellow, green and blue.

'What is all that?' I growl.

'Confusing us,' mutters Frog who has shrapnel splinters in one arm but he won't leave his gun.

'Sodding bloody Highlanders,' growls Pig. 'Off playing their sodding bagpipes somewhere.'

More likely on some crossroads getting wrong directions from a staff officer. But we have held up so far. Twenty-two dead or wounded. A Company next to us is in worse shape.

We eat, try to sleep. Funny how you can't when you're really tired. The Germans must be tired, but there's lots of fight left in them. For that matter, there's a lot left in us.

'We held them, eh?' comes a sudden voice. Creel, looking pale in the flarelight. I bet I know what *his* canteen is full of. 'We'll easily hold them tomorrow, eh, captain?'

'If the Highlanders get here,' says Rowlands.

'They will, they will,' mutters Creel. His eyes flicker, he wants any reason to be out of here.

'Don't worry, sir,' I give him a big cheerful grin, 'if I see any bugger running, I'll shoot him myself.'

Creel gets the message, the yellow rabbit, mutters something to Rowlands and heads on down the trench. I watch him reach the communications sap. He looks back, sees me looking and heads on to the C Company strongpoint.

Rowlands has got the message too. His face is blue-white from the overhead flares, a bar of black shadow cut by his helmet rim. 'I don't want to see anything like that, sergeant.'

'All right, sir. You won't.'

He wouldn't, he was right about that.

We have done whatever trench repairs we can. Puha and Soames snooze together on the firing step while other men huddle in the dugouts. Little Frog, spectacles on the end of his nose, is by the Vickers. He should be working in his father's grocery shop. Pig, the farmer's son; me, the railway ganger. Only war brought us together, and soon the war will be over.

Jessica Collingwood was right. I doubt if I'll see her again.

You'll get your mucking head shot off!

I can't sleep, so I walk down the trenchline. The patched sandbags are in place and there are men sitting on the firing-step, helmeted heads knocking together as they doze.

There's a smell in the air that I know. Fresh blood and raw flesh, the familiar groans and cries from no-man's land. But the Germans are still there, they will look after their own. There's no stink of rotting bodies — no time for it to come in this battle.

It's nearly dawn. The last flares go up and burst into bright colours, red into blue, yellow into green.

I go down the trench, nudging men, kicking the firing-step. There are no rations up today. They huddle in their greatcoats; watching me, the legendary

Sergeant Moran. I know the stories they tell and most of them are crap. They don't know what goes on inside me. The gut-wrenching fear that I have now, that I always have before battle.

If they survive this — and the war — they will forget me. No matter, because I don't want to survive.

It's lighter overhead now. I'm not sleepy and I go through my pockets and chuck out bits of food, spare socks, everything but bandages and my bullets. I press my thumb hard on the tip of my lucky bullet.

Faith!

I'm at the end of the trench now, by the communications sap. The splash of boots and clatter of duckboards comes from ahead. Creel appears, pausing as he sees me by his only exit. I give him a blank scowl. He's not brave enough to call my bluff and goes on up the trench to A Company. Poor bugger.

Poor bugger? Did I say that? He'll find another hole. I won't see him again. A last flare explodes in hissing blue. In the distance, a field-gun goes off. Rowlands is leaning against the back wall of the trench, his eyes shut. Opens them, gives a tired little smile. 'Let's just pray for the Highlanders,' he says. 'Captain Nixon of A Company is down with a head wound. So I'll have to be there as well as here. Means more work for you, sergeant.'

'Yes, sir.'

'I'll get you a battlefield commission if I survive.'

I grin. The fear is gone. 'You do that, sir, and *you* won't survive.'

He laughs. 'All right, old son, do your best.'

We shake hands and he goes off down the line. Our field-guns open. Out of the half-light ahead, German guns reply. Then all hell and cannon-thunder breaks loose; under that, the crackle of small arms fire and I'm shouting.

'Here they come!'

Here they bloody come!

The thunder grows, like a storm building. This storm is iron and lead and the Huns are still out there in no-man's land. A lot of them are on the wire, a lot dead. But there's more massing in the shell-holes and soon their stormtroopers will be at us. First their artillery again, to soften us up — not that we need it.

With shouts and bugles, the Hun infantry attack.

I've never seen anything like that, Frog on the Vickers, his broken spectacles bouncing up and down on his button nose. Shooting, he traverses the gun one side to the other. Beside him Pig feeds the belts of ammo. There's a jam and Frog yells actual swear words as he clears it. Puha is swearing too as he works his Enfield, the same two words over and over again.

I sight the Mannlicher and find a German soldier bellying forward. It's an easy shot but I don't want him, or his mate who's about to throw a grenade. Then two, who're setting up a machine-gun. Crack — crack! The gunner falls across his gun, the loader tangles in his own belts and rolls over.

Seeking, tracking. An officer with binoculars; he falls back. Then bullets hit the sandbags around me, flinging specks of sand into my eyes. I drop back, curse, splash water to rub them clear. Someone grabs my arm. Captain Rowlands.

'Orders to hold at all costs, sergeant. Know what that means?'

Yes, I sodding do! It means some general twelve miles back wants this patch of mud held. It means we all die but we knew that. So I grin at him like it's funny and he grins back. 'Got anything to drink?'

There's some French plonk in my canteen. I'm handing it to him and he's thrown it sharply back, shoulder and chest all bloody, already slipping down.

I turn to see a German storm trooper on the parapet. *How did he get so close?* His face is muddy, his teeth are bared and he's shifting his light machine-gun towards me. I swing up my rifle and shoot from the hip. The German is flung back as the bullet catches under his throat.

'Keep your heads up, muckers!' I scream.

But he was one man, too damn brave for his own good. The others are still pinned down, letting their numbers build for the rush.

Rowlands has sunk to the ground, his face white

as chalk, bright red blood all over his body now. 'Highlanders won't get here in time,' he whispers.

I nod, looks like it.

'Fall back,' he says weakly, 'not enough now to make a difference — not worth more lives.'

'You know we can't do that.'

He tries to speak again and his head falls forward. He might still be alive so I order him taken to his dugout. Take his Webley revolver, rip the lanyard off; they're crap for officers.

I don't remember the next two hours, just bits of it. I remember thumping the men, cursing them up and down the trench to stay put. Once on the parapet, firing my Mannlicher and being pulled back. The Germans come closer, their potato-masher bombs landing in the trench. We throw them back, Soames too late, one blows his arm off. Puha is next — a bullet in the face.

Down to forty men and no sign of the bloody Highlanders.

We hear German bugles — they are attacking again. We fire over the parapet, working rifles as fast as we can reload. I grab Puha's Enfield for the 'Mad Minute' routine. *Like riding a bike!* Closer and closer, like the Turks at Chunuk Bair, you can see their faces as you kill them. See the bullet holes. And once more the grey ranks fall back or fall dead, take cover.

And as they fall back a lull comes like when the

rain eases. I shout, 'B Company, too damn tough, eh?' They cheer back, the mud-stained bloody heroes; never mind I've been kicking and cursing them.

Not many of us left now. Soames has bled to death. Pig is torn apart by shrapnel, tears in Frog's eyes as he covers the body with his overcoat. I splash up and down the trenchline, trying to think what Rowlands would say. But I don't have his turn of phrase. Just say we are Fernleaves, En-Zedders, Aussies are holding so we have to, no damn Hun is kicking us out. And not because some Chateau-Charlie told us to.

They listen, some even cheer. Bloody, covered with filth, most wounded. But reloading magazine clips, levering the lid off the last grenade crates. We're staying because we want to and will go down fighting.

'About five hundred rounds left for the Vickers,' says Frog.

'Bad news. You're a piss-poor rifle shot.'

I grin and he grins back. Five hundred rounds, we'll be through that in a few minutes. Bullets sleeting like hail as the storm rebuilds, shells scream and crash. Someone comes blundering down the line, Creel, the sleeve of his overcoat in rags, mudstained, but no wounds.

He blunders into me, makes to pass. His face is white, I grab him and shout, 'Orders, sir?'

'Orders?'

He looks at me, his eyes vacant, breathing

heavily. Sure the German guns have laid down a full load but that's not battle-shock. It's simple, gutless fear.

'A Company's nearly gone,' he babbles, points confusedly up-trench. I'm checking down here.'

Sure — to where the communication trench is!

'Rowlands is down, sir. I need orders!'

He gasps and gulps, shakes his head. 'I'll find someone — hold on.'

'Don't run, you yellow bastard!'

'Sergeant —' his voice goes shrill as a German screams overhead. 'Oh hell, I didn't want this, my father did — understand?' He's grabbing my arm, tears in his eyes, sweat trickling down his face. 'Find some-one, back soon —'

And he's blundering off down the trench, still holding his binoculars. His cap falls off but he doesn't stop. Click — click, as I reload the Mannlicher and drop to one knee, that icy hot rage kicking inside me again. *He thinks we want it?*

'Jacko!'

Shut up, Frog — interfere and you are dead! You don't like Creel, nobody does. He's at the end now, he should fork left into C Company's trenches, but in a moment, he blunders into the communication trench.

He's quick, with all the rabbit speed of the coward — but not as quick as me. The rifle cracks in my ears, the butt thumps my shoulder. Creel jerks, scrabbles at the sandbagged side then falls into the communication trench. I can see his booted legs sticking out, they kick and go still. Those nice shiny boots.

I look back. The others are watching, no expression on their faces. The mud plasters them like war-paint. I don't know if they approve and don't care. Frog just loads a belt onto his Vickers and the battle comes around us again. We are back in the storm, Creel forgotten as the Germans come again. Rank after rank and not enough of us to hold them.

Mucking idiot, get your mucking head — you couldn't hold a trench like this, you old bastard!

Brody is next, flopping dead. There's shrapnel whizzing everywhere, there's blood on me. A shellburst kills two more, stripping uniform and flesh from their bodies. Those stick-handled bombs sailing over, one lands on the sandbags before me. Grab the handle, throw it back; it explodes as I duck and bits whang off the flat brim of my helmet. Shrapnel cuts, bleeding, don't feel them.

Maybe twenty left, all wounded.

B Company is dying on its feet.

More bombs sail over and a man howls, his leg shattered. Frog yells for the last ammo belt — then Frog is dead, his chest smashed by bullets. I pull him off the gun, connect the belt and grab the firing handles. That rage, hot rage, cold rage —

You're going to know it was Todeshund!

So stand up now, nothing matters, the long snout

of the Vickers over the parapet and blaze away — like I'm forcing out anger with the bullets. *The Huns are too close!* No anger for them, just for me — as though I'm killing because I don't know a damned thing. Yes, and because of Rowlands, Brasso, Frog, *Eileen!*

The Huns are closer and closer as I swing the gun. Some fold or spin around. The last bullets click through and the Vickers falls silent. Now, grey-uniformed soldiers leap down into our trench, my blokes meet them with clubbed rifles.

There's Huns coming and I bang away with Rowlands' revolver. A German comes at me, his snarl fixed, bayonet out. Smack it away, bash him with the butt of my Mannlicher. More ahead, jostled from behind. Too many, time to die. I turn, bayonet out, a red-whiskered man backhands me.

'Hoots mon, are ye daft?'

The Highlanders! They are splashing up the trenchline to start a short vicious fight. The Germans inside our trench are shot or bayoneted. One jumps over the parapet and screams as he is stuck on a bayonet. The officers shout orders, manning the firing-steps, jostling our few men aside. The full mad roar of rifle-fire is like the storm renewed.

I know — *know* — the Germans will not stand for this. They're as near to breaking as we are. I lean back, aware my left arm is hurting like it's broken, and red from shoulder to sleeve.

An officer — a bloody schoolboy — stops. 'Dashed good work, sergeant, pull your men out.'

There's just about none left to pull out, I want to say, but he's gone down the trench, shouting orders. Already the rifle-storm seems less because the Huns are beaten back. The only grey uniforms in the trench are on dead bodies. The kilties arrived just in time.

They work their Enfields like the bloody good soldiers they are and swear their strange oaths. There's even a bagpipe going somewhere. Those kilts like damned skirts, 'ladies from hell' the Huns call them. Right now I'd rather see these ladies than all the painted dames in the Black Lily.

A slow painful slog to the second-line trenches. Of our battalion, about two hundred survivors. The Huns threw some ten thousand men against us. Most of them stayed in no-man's land.

A doctor dressed my arm, bruised by a rifle-butt and cut with shell fragments. It would only mean a week or two out of the line, but we're being pulled back anyway. All of us like sleepwalkers, hands shaking so badly, we almost can't hold our rifles.

Fields comes up, muddy as us all, a bandage around his head because he's a fighting colonel. 'Where's Major Creel?' he asks.

Before I can answer, an A Company boy says how they found him in the communication trench —

wounded. Foolishly they brought him back. And Shaw, the born fool, pipes up.

'He came through our trench, sir, a Hun bullet got him by the sap.'

'The communication sap?' asks Fields, frowning.

'Seemed in a hurry, sir,' says another, Ward. And, clueless as Shaw, adds, 'A Hun bullet, sir, for sure.'

Fields nods. He glances at my Mannlicher, then at me. But he says nothing, then or later. Maybe with his battalion shot to pieces and good officers like Rowlands and Nixon dead or wounded, it doesn't matter so much.

The Hun offensive grinds to a stop at Amiens.

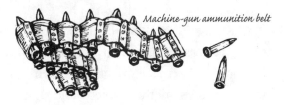

Machine-gun ammunition belt

New Zealand, 1940

HELL, IT'S dark now. Getting black when it should be getting light. There's a noise, like a rat in the dugout. Me, my hand moving, rustling the white starched sheets. Can't see these either, lungs all full now — something groaning and rattling like a broken engine — my breath.

Amiens is where I lost all my mates. They gave me the DSO and some French medal, the *Croix de* something. A French general kissed me on both cheeks. Luckily I'd shaved.

By September, the Germans were cracked, their last strength gone. We were nearly as beaten, but they didn't have endless Yank divisions coming by the shipload.

Amiens wasn't the end. We turned the Germans back but they tried once more, another big offensive. We fought them at Messines and other places. I woke up in a dressing station, my lungs on fire. I never saw my Mannlicher again; or my lucky bullet.

I'M SITTING IN the grounds of this hospital, my lungs better. An American doctor says I'll be 'OK soon and fit as a fiddle.' There's a lot of American nurses who speak at the tops of their voices and give us round cakes with a hole in the middle — 'dough-nuts'.

I'm lucky to be here. An epidemic called Spanish influenza is raging now, killing better than the Germans, spreading all over Europe and in Britain too, and there's nothing the doctors can do.

'Good morning, sergeant. I'm leaving France tomorrow.'

And up comes Jessica Collingwood in grey uniform and cape. She sits down like we were old mates who saw each other every day.

'Major Creel's on the same ship. They're still picking splinters out of his thigh and his backside's missing a chunk. He's going to remember Amiens every time he sits down.'

Of course she's heard the rumours — Shaw is a blabbermouth. I just give her a blank look and she smiles like it's the answer she's expecting. She lights a cigarette. I'm not allowed to yet — the gas.

'You won't see combat again, Jacko. Word is the Kaiser will abdicate, so that's the end.' A short bitter laugh. 'Until the next war of course.'

'This is the war to end all wars, remember?'

She laughs again. 'I'm sure they'll say that about the next one.' She blows out a smoke ring and says something I don't understand. 'We're both snipers, Jacko. What the hell will society do with us?'

'What the hell does it matter?'

Off on that bloody hobby-horse of hers again.

'Jacko, you showed courage and leadership. With a good education, you could have been somebody.'

'With a decent father —'

'You used your hate of him to stay alive. But you may still end up like him. So will the slums be levelled and the poor get what they need?'

'You sound like a Red. One of those — what were they? — Bolshies.'

She shakes her head wearily. 'I'm not even a bloody socialist. Oh, there'll be some changes, hand-tailored so the status quo won't be disturbed.'

One of the American nurses yells something and Jessica looks over. 'You know what delayed the Yanks? The British shipping barons were dickering for more money, including full payment if a ship was sunk. A Yank colonel who got his foot shot off told me.'

'The top bastards have always been like that.'

She stubs out her cigarette — the smell was driving me mad. She leans forward, looking intense now. 'Jacko, you were sniping at Germans, I was sniping at society. We were proving what we could do.'

'We did prove that.' What the *hell* was she on about?

'Yes,' she's still intense, 'but our real battle was with the people who sent us to die. And not for Empire and King. For their own interests — to make money from a war they could have ended when they liked by letting the Germans back out with dignity — a bloody phone call to Berlin was all it took!'

'Things have to bloody change now.'

'No they won't. Your medals will be worth their scrap-metal value.' There are tears on her cheek now. 'I lost the man I loved at Gallipoli. I've seen lovers, sons, husbands, fathers, mutilated or patched up to go back and die. Good women too. And I have an awful, horrible fear that it was for nothing.'

Then she uses some swear words, real shockers.

So loud that even the American nurses stop talking and look over. She sits there, her head in her hands, then looks up, cheeks wet with tears. 'All for nothing.'

'Can I look you up when I get home?'

She gets up. 'Why not? Both snipers, might form an association. Do take care of yourself, Jacko.'

Her eyes are bright with tears too. She squeezes my hand and walks off without looking back. I would like her to, but she doesn't. Goes through a door and it shuts.

She shipped home on the cruise-ship *Niagara* but the Spanish influenza went back on the ship with them. Quarantine? Forget it, the leaders of our war-time coalition government were on board. So the influenza got ashore and seven thousand New Zealanders died.

Nurse Jessica Collingwood, doing volunteer work in Auckland Hospital, was among the first.

She didn't live long enough to realise that everything she said was true. Nobody gave a damn.

Last time I saw Jessica was nearly the end of my war too.

'You know what they did?' asks Brasso. 'Put a couple of bloody marbles in my eyes — where my eyes used to be. Says it'll help keep the shape of my eyelids. Nice of them, eh Jacko?'

I'm on sick-leave before rejoining my company. The armistice was signed yesterday and the guns are silent. Brasso's going to be shipped to a big new place for blind soldiers in England. There's a lot of them now.

'We had some Bible-basher around.' Brasso has a flat way of speaking now, not the old excited yak-yak. 'He says we can do all kinds of useful work — like weaving baskets. Some bloody institution will look after us for the rest of our lives. Nice, eh?'

'Sorry, Brasso.' I've already said that a few times.

'Then he asked what we were good at.'

'What'd you say?'

'Cards.'

'Not whist, mate, remember?' Not the brightest thing to say because it makes us think of Frog.

Brasso doesn't smile and there's nothing else to say because all we had in common was the war. And that's over.

He's playing with his cards as we talk. Shuffling, reshuffling, the silver card-case open beside him. Even blind he doesn't lose a card.

The visiting bell goes and I have to leave. Brasso puts up a hand to stop me. 'Jacko, describe this bloody room, will you? Why is there air on my face?'

We're on the second floor with the window open to a small balcony outside. The walls are army white-wash and there are blue curtains. A bedside table, his kit on a chair. It's bleak and somehow smells that way. Brasso will be asking questions like that for the rest of his life.

'Thanks, mate,' he says, a spark of the old Brasso. 'Just like to know where I am.'

'I'll come tomorrow. We'll keep in touch.'

'Sure, Jacko. Tomorrow.'

I do go back the next day. The orderly who comes over is another one of those well-fed backline soldiers, who sounds smug as he tells me Brasso is dead. 'Found him under his window. Neck broken, of course. Took the coward's way out —'

He stops because I have him tight by the collar. A nurse is coming up and a voice I know asks me to let go. I turn. It's Betty Donaghy. She doesn't seem surprised to see me.

I give the orderly a little shake, release him and he totters away. Betty tells me quietly what happened. Brasso got out of bed last night, opened the window I described to him, went out on the balcony and over it.

I have to sit down. Losing Brasso is the very end, but I know why he did it. He was frightened of darkness, like I was scared of peace. I tell her that and she nods, she understands. She's a good nurse now, way past showing emotion.

'I know what you want to do,' she says calmly. 'Knock that orderly's teeth out, and I should let you.

But it won't change anything. I'll deal with him. Brasso scribbled a note, wanted you to have these.'

His silver card-case and deck of cards. Betty walks with me to the door. The orderly is nowhere to be seen. Betty takes my hand at the door.

'Jessica told me why you broke us up. You were right to, anyway. I knew nothing about war or soldiers, or how I would change. Goodbye, Jacko.'

A year on, she's got Jessica Collingwood's look in her eyes now. Nothing will surprise her.

'Goodbye, Betty.'

Just like I'd said, 'Bye, Brasso', yesterday. Two more lives out of mine because I never saw her again either.

I lost the card-case at poker. Kings and aces against a Running Flush. Brasso would have laughed like hell.

One more hospital. They all smell of carbolic soap and bring back painful memories. This one was more of a convalescent home for wounded officers.

Rowlands is in a room with two others — one in a wheelchair with dark glasses and no legs, the other on his bed, looks asleep, an empty sleeve pinned over his dressing-gown.

Rowlands looks about ten years older. There's pain lines on his face but he manages a smile. He has an empty sleeve too, and most of the shoulder missing as well.

'Hello, sergeant. Glad you came.'

He might be, but there's no war now. So, like Brasso, not much to talk about. He's going home. Jokes about him and the sleeping officer setting up in business. One good right arm, one good left. Maybe set up as a typist between them; or learn knitting. I smile but we both know they're bad jokes.

'Some Hun marksman was damned clever to get Creel inside the trench like that,' he says. 'Bloody good shot, eh, Jacko?'

That's about the only time he called me 'Jacko'. He's going back to the family department store; you can manage a business one-handed. When I go, he won't let me salute. Grips my hand tight and says to look him up in New Zealand.

I don't look him up. We never see each other again.

And what did he mean, bloody good shot? Bloody *bad* shot, hitting Creel in his backside.

I was aiming for his head.

Going back to New Zealand didn't seem real. The trenches and the mud; the bullets and stink of rotting bodies — they were real. Well-dressed people in busy

231

streets, their homes not shattered by shellfire; they were not real. My whole street was being knocked flat to build new houses.

I met Ellen once, fat as Mum with her third kid on the way. She hadn't seen Kate for years. People saying, we know what you boys went through, but we had rationing and this killer flu — *so we didn't have it easy, lads!*

I went to see Frog's parents. They were little be-spectacled people like him. And very proud that Sergeant Moran, fearless stalker of Huns and Victoria Cross winner, came to see them. They wanted me to come back but I made excuses.

Pig's mum and dad too. They offered me a place on the farm, but I couldn't look at green fields without seeing shell-craters. Or muddy ground without sweating. There were hens clucking when Duncan was shot. I didn't go back there either.

The nightmares came. Fighting up to my neck in corpses and black mud. Firing that Vickers to stop the Huns at Amiens. But it was jamming, parts kept falling off, the Huns closer and *closer* —

Getting chucked out of my boarding-house, landlady says I'm screaming in my sleep. A word sounding like Tottund, Tottund …

I began drinking. The only way to sleep was to knock myself out. I even got married. Alice, nice girl, shop assistant. She fell in love with Jacko the war hero, not me. The booze and the nightmares went on; we broke up after the first kid. She went to her parents, and we haven't seen each other since.

I got jobs, at least Jacko the war hero did. Moran, the peace-time drunk, lost them in a week. Then the Depression came and I ended up in a work camp. It was a bit like the army, bad food, do as you're told. After that, I went on the road.

I was coughing a lot then. A doc said I should stop drinking and stop thinking about the war. *Nightmares of blood and black slime* — how do I stop those?

I met blokes I'd known in the army. Some had adjusted just by shutting the war out, and some were on the road like me. I sold my VC for three quid — enough for a few days' bender.

Creel went into politics. Of course people voted for an army officer, limping from his honourable wound. He greased his way up to a top political job. He gave a talk at our work camp once how Government wished it could do more. Told about me, he came up with a big smile and his hand outstretched. I spat on the ground.

He's an Associate-something in this wartime coalition government too — done all right for himself, his type always do. But I bet he thinks of me every time he sits down. Even on my worst days, that's still worth a smile.

I don't remember much about the last years. Drinking, drunk and disorderly, sleeping rough, in and out of jail. War couldn't kill me but the bloody peace did. It just took a hell of a long time.

Victoria Cross

New Zealand, 1940

SO ... FINALLY, THIS place. This morning that should be light but is dark as memory.

'We did some things right. We did hold the line,' comes Jessica's voice from somewhere.

Yeah, and now there's another war and people like us will fight it; bleed and die to hold the line. Oh God, it must get better. I wish I could go and fight and live again.

Too dark now. I'm glad the trench doesn't stink the way it used to. My mind is drifting now like flares, colours of darkness in no-man's land. I have to go out once more but I'm not afraid.

People at my bed, I blink awake. An old man, white-haired, in black, intoning something — screw religion, mate, no God in the trenches *— a younger man, boy, looking at me, strained and scared. He's like me.*

My son! Stay away, you stupid bugger. I bet your mum told you not to come *— me saying a word, the phlegm bubbling —* Faith, *what is that? Blackness, boy gone, the priest's intoning lost in darkness, no moon tonight.*

Is that you, Nurse Bondi, who is sinking? Are you actually crying? I'm not sinking, I'm going out on night patrol. With my Mannlicher rifle and my lucky bullet — Faith. *I'll be all right in the darkness.*

I hunt there. I belong there.